MEMOIRS
of a BOOKBAT

Kathryn Lasky

HARCOURT, INC.

SAN DIEGO   NEW YORK   LONDON

Requests for permission to make copies of any part of the work
should be mailed to the following address: Permissions Department,
Harcourt, Inc., 6277 Sea Harbor Drive, Orlando, Florida 32887-6777.

Excerpt from *Jump! The Adventures of Brer Rabbit* by Joel Chandler
Harris, copyright © 1986 by Van Dyke Parks and Malcolm Jones,
reprinted by permission of Harcourt, Inc.

Excerpt from "Bats" by Randall Jarrell, reprinted by permission of
Mary Jarrell, Executrix of Estate of Randall Jarrell.

First Harcourt, Inc. paperback edition 1996

Library of Congress Cataloging-in-Publication Data
Lasky, Kathryn.
Memoirs of a bookbat/Kathryn Lasky.
p.   cm.
Summary: Fourteen-year-old Harper, an avid reader, looks back on
her life and realizes that her parents' public promotion of censorship
has grown into a quest for control over her choices and decisions.
ISBN 0-15-215727-1
ISBN 0-15-201259-1 (pbk.)
[1. Censorship—Fiction.   2. Books and reading—Fiction.]
I. Title.
PZ7.L3274Mc   1994
[Fic]—dc20   93-36402

Text set in Galliard.
Designed by Lydia D'moch

J I H G F E D C B A
M L K J I H G F E D   (pbk.)

Printed in the Unites States of America

For Max,
who reads with passion

PROLOGUE

The funny thing about Gray is his name. He's not gray at all. He is—with his sharp blue eyes, standout freckles, and red hair, Georgia-dirt red hair, that's what I call it—full of color. And besides all that he is one of the most opinionated people I know.

Gray has this craziness about him, and in a sense that's how my troubles began. But really, I think—I know—that trouble had been coming for a long time. Granted, it probably wouldn't have been as interesting without Gray. It still would have been scary, though, and sooner or later I would have wound up where I am right now, on a bus in the middle of nowhere, with this awful knot in my stomach.

Gray Willette is the best friend I have ever had. And I haven't had all that many.

For the last four years, from about fifth grade until now, I had never been in one school long enough to do a whole term project, let alone make a really close friend. A lot of places I never even got a report card because my little sister, Weesie, and I hardly ever spent more than six weeks in one school district. At first I thought the moving was OK, because things got so much better around the time we started traveling.

For one thing, we got a much nicer trailer with a really quiet generator. The generator was important to Mom. She said the old one sounded like a clothes dryer with a load of marbles and tin cans. The noise never bothered me much. It just became what they call white noise. It screened out loud talking and everything else from inside the trailer and all the babies crying and folks yelling outside in the trailer court. It meant I could read in peace.

No doubt about it, reading saved me back then. Friends were hard to make when I knew I'd have to pick up and leave every month or so, but it was sure different with books. In Arkansas they were doing base ten problems in math in the sixth grade; then when we got to Missouri they were still having kids draw pies with slices to explain fractions. Every new classroom was different, but I could always count on the library to be familiar. The call numbers don't change. 910 is always geography whether I'm in Oklahoma City or Kokomo, Indiana. 398 is folktales, 560 is dinosaurs, and 549 is rocks and minerals. Even the gerbils in the cage by the checkout desk are always the same. Those little rodents get the same eczema in California that they get in Tennessee and Nebraska.

It got even better when I discovered interlibrary loan. Any book I wanted could follow me wherever I went. Nothing stumps the public library system. My notion at this point is that librarians should take over the postal system and Social Security. Gray says that's stretching it, but as long as I'm stretching it, he says, why not have them run the Defense Department, too?

I met Gray at the Spoonwood Public Library in California. I had read my way out of the children's room and into the science fiction shelves upstairs. The first time I ever saw him, I was standing in the section labeled ScF Edd. I was just starting David Eddings' Belgariad series; Book One wasn't in, so I was considering Book Two, *Queen of Sorcery*. Gray was about six feet away at ScF Mac, looking at Delores Macuccho, the foremost master of horror fiction—but we just call her Delores.

It's hard not to think about Gray. He said before he helped me pile on this bus not to worry—he'd see me sometime not too far off. I don't know. When I look out the window of the bus speeding along, I know that with every mile I'm farther away from Gray. And I'm farther away from my parents, from Weesie, and from all the trouble, too.

I *won't* think about it. If I do, I'll either get mad or start feeling sorry for myself. I can see my reflection in the window. My hair is a mess. I can't exactly wash it on a bus. It's gotten all frizzy. Dirty blond frizz—a noncolor, as far as I'm concerned. And my too-small eyes are a wash-out gray-green. My nose is small, too, and so is my mouth. And this wouldn't be a problem except that my face is too big. So all my stupid features don't look delicate and feminine at all. They just look stranded on a desert of pale freckles. Charming!

I press my cheek against the cool glass. I can almost feel the rain streaking down it, the rivulets flattened into thin sheets, blurring the view outside. I like this landscape. Just wheatfields somewhere in Kansas, the wheat still young and thin, no ugly billboards, no mile markers to remind me of fixed points. I'm suspended in this wet, glazed world of wheat and sky, pressed into a moving watercolor. I'm a wet streak on the paper. Shapes shift, colors change. Nothing is dry, nothing is set. It can all wash away in an instant.

It's been clear to me for a long time that my family's moving around—and the reason behind it—pretty much wrecked my life, but Mom always says I should be more grateful. Migrant laborers' kids have it worse than Weesie and I ever did. All those pickers in the Napa and San Joaquin valleys, or out around Castroville, artichoke capital of the world, they're just picking grapes and artichokes and strawberries. My family picks something more, something for the everlasting. Mom says we're not just migrant laborers—we're migrants for God.

1

AN ENDLESS NIGHT

There was a time, before the trailer, when we lived in a house that stayed in one place. Weesie wasn't born yet. I think we had a little patch of yard, and I know there was a sprinkler because I can remember my dad turning it on for me to play in. One time it squirted him right in the face, so he just decided to let it sprinkle him, clothes and all, and we both stood there and laughed.

Then we moved. I had been all excited because Mom said we were moving into a house on wheels and I thought that was really funny. I don't think it was funny for Mom and Dad. Something had happened with Dad's job, and it was cheaper to live in the trailer, I guess. But my mom was trying to make the trailer seem like a great adventure. Putting a good face on it, which is OK. Sometimes you have to do that.

"You mean the house is going to roll, Mom?" I asked.

"Yes, darling."

"You mean everything inside of it rolls with it?"

"Yes, ma'am, everything."

"You mean the beds go traveling?"

"Yes, ma'am."

"And the stove?"

"Yes, ma'am."

"And the kitchen table and the refrigerator and the sink and the bathroom?"

"Yes ma'am, yes ma'am, yes ma'am, and yes ma'am." She laughed and gave me a squeeze. But her laugh was kind of tight and she hugged me a little bit too hard.

I thought the whole notion of a rolling house was wonderful, almost like a magic carpet. I was wrong. The rolling house was a small dark tunnel with one little window on each side, and the bathroom always smelled. For a long time we never rolled anywhere. We were plugged into a trailer court on the edge of some town, and there was a neon pizza sign across the highway that blinked off and on and filled one window with its red ZZs. I could see that window from my bed, and I used to stare at it at night when I couldn't sleep because of Dad's yelling. And Mom would be whimpering.

They might as well have both been screaming bloody murder because it tears up whoever is listening all the same. But it is not my mom's style to yell. Whenever Dad got upset, Mom would always try to act calm first, and she'd tell him that nothing was as bad as it seemed. Then she would be super sweet. Not that she didn't mean it, but she just laid it on so thick sometimes that it would make Dad get worse. And when he did get madder, then finally, but not often, she might start screaming back.

I don't really remember what my dad's jobs were before he started driving for the bus company. He had been spending a lot of time at home, so I guess he was out of work. Then he got the bus-driving job and things got better for a while—until the accident. I'll never forget that night. I was seven years old.

———

"It's going to work out, Hank. They've got insurance. You know what Mr. Foster said. It was the old lady's fault. She just walked right out there against the light."

"Oh, this is all very easy for you to say, Beth. You don't know how these people operate." His voice, a low hiss, scalded the close air of the trailer and cut right through my sleep. I opened one eye. The ZZs were blinking in the window.

"They can't blame you for something that you didn't do intentionally."

This was the way it always started out—Mom trying to be so understanding and Dad so full of anger. Sometimes I thought it would be better if she just started right off yelling.

"Now, now, Hank," she said softly.

"Don't do that!" Of course I never said it, and her soothing voice went on. I heard her get up and walk across to him. "Don't!" I shouted silently. She was going to stroke his hair. I knew it.

Then he mumbled something about going out, and she barked, "No!" From my bed I could see their shadows dancing across the ceiling.

"Get out of the way!" my dad yelled.

The shadows were knotted up around the

doorway and then I heard a yelp. I leaned way out of bed to peek through my doorway to the front of the trailer. Dad was gone, and Mom was just standing there, holding her mouth. I knew in an instant what had happened. As if to confirm it, Mom kicked the half-open door as hard as she could. It slammed shut.

"Damn door," she muttered. It had swung back and knocked her in the mouth.

She stuffed her face into a dish towel and the generator kicked in right on cue to blanket her whimpers. Full of rattles and sputters, it made a good cover. We could all be separate and private, hiding within its din. But suddenly the noise stopped. I heard my dad come back into the trailer.

"We can't afford to run this stupid generator. You're just going to have to be hot." His voice was hoarse.

Most of the power came from the trailer court, but if we wanted to run air conditioning, we had to do it from our own generator because of something to do with power overloads and brownouts. What I did understand was that it cost us more when we ran the generator, so whenever Dad got mad about money he yanked out the plug. He'd come back only to shut it off. Then he left again. Mom didn't dare turn it back on.

The night was long and hot and sweaty. I heard my mom whimpering, and I heard my dad come back in later. I knew he'd been drinking. I hoped he'd get so hot he would turn the generator back on, not for the coolness as much as for the noise, but he didn't. He just mumbled through the night. Then I heard him whimpering, and the night seemed never to end, and we were all there in the awful darkness and the thick, quiet heat, exposed and bare with all our sores showing and the two red ZZs blinking dumbly. I wanted suddenly to be a bird, to spiral out into the night and fly high above the ZZs, to fling myself into the wind. In the morning, if morning ever came, I knew I would see a welt across my mom's face and then pretend not to see it. I shut my eyes tight. Inside my eyelids the glaring neon still danced its red-hot jig.

Morning did come, and there was a red dent, the exact shape of the door's edge, from Mom's cheek to her chin. Her swollen lips looked like a mashed-up dark blossom. I didn't notice until later that one of her front teeth was chipped. I could pretend that I didn't see the dent, and I could have pretended that I didn't see the chip, but before I thought about it I blurted out, "Mom, what happened to your tooth?"

Her hands flew to her mouth. Behind her fingers her face looked like it was collapsing, and I suddenly got really scared. I thought that if she took her hand away there would be a dark emptiness that her face had fallen into. Her eyes were big, as if they were watching something terrible, a private kind of terribleness that I wasn't supposed to see. Then she turned and ran out, slamming the trailer door.

It was the sound I'd heard when she had kicked the door shut that night and cursed it. I suddenly saw the instant after the yelp; I saw the white splinters fly through the hot, dark air. When I had asked her about the tooth it was as if she had been hit again—as if I had hit her. We had all been so careful, me, my dad, and my mom, not to notice the mark the door had left on Mom's face. They thought I had been asleep, or they were at least pretending I was. And I had been pretending. I made my own generator noise inside my head, and so did Mom, whenever Dad pulled the plug. We created the rattles and thonks so we

13

wouldn't have to listen to anything else. And Dad, he went out and he drank, and the drinking made him mumble instead of roar. But now I had spoiled it all.

I had a sudden terrible urge to look for those little tooth fragments. I dropped down on my knees and began crawling around. I wanted to fit everything back together, but I was crying so hard I couldn't really see the floor. All the dust and grit and dirt we'd tracked into the trailer blurred. I'd never find any of the pieces. I dug the heels of my palms into my eyes until I saw stars, then I looked up and out the window. It was still daylight. Weesie was in her highchair chasing a Cheerio around in a puddle of milk on her tray. She was so little she didn't have to pretend anything. I envied Weesie at that moment, I really did. I was seven years old, but I desperately wanted to be just a little baby.

So in the beginning there was the pretending.

2

GOLDILOCKS, I AM

It's hard for me to remember everything I read back then, but I do remember *The Three Little Pigs*. Not that I was into pigs. I was into houses—houses that weren't shaped like shoeboxes, houses without wheels. I didn't care if the houses were made from twigs or straw or bricks; I just hated the one we lived in, so I liked reading about other places. And I remember reading about weather, rain in particular. It had been very hot and dry for a long time, as it can get in Texas, and I had found a book of weather poems. There was a poem about rain that I especially loved when it was really hot. Something about the rhythm and the way those words dropped into your mind sounded just like the plink of raindrops.

My dad was still working for the bus company, but they had taken him off as a driver and put him on a desk job. He hated it. Then one day he came home late. Mom had already given Weesie and me supper. I know I had been reading the plinking poem that day because now I remember how funny it was the way it all worked out—how the sounds of the poem were in my head and then it really did rain.

I was on the couch in the trailer with the cool plinks dropping like silver in my head when suddenly there was an awful slam and the whole trailer shook. Dad had driven our car right into the hitch, which we had on our trailer even though we never hitched on to anything to go anyplace. Mom screamed and Weesie started to cry. I peeked over the edge of the book and saw Mom close her eyes tight and grip her hands together at her heart. Her hands were clenched, but something else in her relaxed. A calm washed over her, and with it came strength. I wasn't afraid. I put down the book to watch what would happen next.

"It's over!" Dad said in a thick voice as he stormed through the door.

"You lost the desk job," Mom said calmly. There was something new in her voice. I could see by the way Dad looked at her that he heard it, too. And I could tell that she wasn't going to do her usual comforting routine. She wasn't going to be mean or anything. I still believe that my mother could never be intentionally mean. But on this night she just stood there, calm and strong as anything. My dad started to sit down.

"Don't sit down," she said almost sharply. Her tone seemed to travel right up his backbone; he looked at her and straightened up as if sitting down were the last thing he would ever think of doing. Mom even looked different. She has a roundish chin and used to wear her hair cut straight with bangs, pulled back with a headband. She looked kind of young for a wife and mother. But suddenly her whole jaw seemed sharper and more angular. Her gray-green eyes, the same washed-out color as mine, were full of glints and sparks. She looked older.

"Hold on, let me get a jacket. It might rain," she said.

Fat chance, I thought, still holding my poem book under my chin.

"Where we going?" Dad asked.

"Church." She grabbed him by the elbow and

steered him out the trailer door. "Take care of Weesie, Harper. We won't be late, and Darla is next door if you need anything."

We had never gone to church all that much. But I knew that my mom had recently met some ladies who belonged to the church a few blocks away. She had met with them for morning coffee and had left Weesie with Darla, I guess. I had been in school. Until then, I hadn't thought very much about it.

The car fender was hooked on the hitch so they had to walk. And, sure enough, it was raining when they came home later that evening. The rain didn't exactly plink in Texas. It went splat on the highway and plonk on the aluminum trailer. Between the splats and the plonks I heard my parents, and they were laughing softly and talking low and sweet to each other. I was in bed, so I peeked around the corner to see them. My dad's shirt stuck to him like drenched tissue paper and my mom's hair was plastered to her head like a glistening dark cap. Their faces were shiny with rain. My mom still looked older, and my dad looked younger. He didn't have those gray pouches under his eyes anymore. And there seemed to be a springiness to his body.

They were kissing and nudging each other as if they were sharing some private joke. I liked it. I felt as if we were all really together for the first time since we moved into the shoebox-on-wheels. I curled up in my bed and hugged my knees. The rain was plonking and Mom and Dad looked all rain-slick and happy. It was OK. It seemed kind of crazy, my dad had lost his job, but it was OK.

They kept going to church, to those prayer meetings on weeknights, and it kept being OK. Dad started going to a men's prayer group in addition to the one for couples they had gone to on that rainy night. Dad seemed happy, even though he still didn't have a regular job. He collected unemployment money and got odd jobs from people he met at the meetings, and he even started doing some stuff for the church. I think he refinished a floor for them and did some tree planting.

Mom started baking again. She was a really good baker. Her specialty was vanilla frosted cookies. The secret was the vanilla bean; she didn't ever use the kind of vanilla that comes in a bottle. Vanilla beans look like stiff old shoe-strings. Gammy, my mom's mom, sent them from Georgia. You open them up and scrape a little of the insides into the batter. I loved it when Mom would come to kiss me good night after she'd been baking. She had this way of holding my face between her hands when she leaned over to give me good-night kisses, and I could smell the vanilla on her hands, so sweet and smooth.

I guess the easy answer to their happiness is that they had found God. But it was different than that, really. I'm not sure whether they'd actually lost God before, anyway. I think it was like they found a group of people to be with and talk to. It might have been the first time they had friends, for all I know.

Looking back, I can see a few tiny changes that give a clue about things to come. I remember one evening when Mom and Dad were at a prayer meeting. Darla had just checked in on us and put Weesie to bed, and I was looking at a new picture book from the library. You could still smell the glue on the little pocket with the date card. The librarian knew I loved any books written and illustrated by Rosemary Nearing, so she'd saved this new one for me. Gammy had sent me a couple of Rosemary Nearing books for my birthday one year. She'd said she couldn't decide which was the prettiest and they were both good stories so she'd just sent the two along. That's my Gammy.

Anyhow, Mom and Dad came home while I was looking at this book. They looked at me and each gave me a quick, tight little smile, and then their eyes clamped on my book like pins on a magnet. I wonder if I felt something turn way down deep inside me then the way I do now, sitting here on this bus almost seven years later. It's hard to forget how they looked at me.

"What's your book?" Dad said. I couldn't find my tongue. So I slid my hands away and let them see the bright, beautiful cover with the little girl in the pinafore and the three fuzzy bears.

"Did Gammy send you this?" Mom asked with that old sweetness that tries to cover things up and make them better.

"No," I said quietly. "I got it at the library."

My parents didn't say anything. I had the strangest feeling, as if I had stumbled into the wrong house, into some place I didn't belong. Someone was about to say, "Who's been sleeping in my bed?" And I thought, *I am Goldilocks, I am!*

3

I WRITE TO THE GOLDILOCKS LADY

My dad picked up the book and leafed through it. Rosemary Nearing drew flowers so you could look right down their throats and see every beautiful little speckle and flower part. But Dad just flipped through like he didn't even notice. I knew it was special that the librarian had saved the book just for me, and I felt sad that the next pair of hands after mine were so careless. I took the book back and held it to my chest.

Then my mom said, "Well, Hank, you know Harper. She's always been kind of bookish." There was the old Mom again, trying to smooth things over, trying to keep everything calm.

"No," I said quickly. I didn't want this to be

a situation that required all that sweet stuff from Mom. And there was some kind of survival instinct operating in me that made me say the next thing, which was a lie. "I don't really like the book that much."

So there we were, back in the pretending business again. I don't know how I knew to lie, but it seemed to satisfy my parents. I didn't like it one bit. I felt as if I had betrayed Rosemary Nearing, the Goldilocks lady, and her book.

It was that guilty feeling nibbling at the edges of my brain that started me on a life of major lying and covering up. It doesn't really make sense. You feel guilty about lying so then you do it some more. You just get better at doing it, so it becomes easier to do and easier to rationalize. You begin to choose when you're going to lie and when you're going to be honest, and you figure out that the honesty outweighs the lies, or at least you tell yourself that.

It was honesty that made me send the letter to Rosemary. Rosemary Nearing was the first author or illustrator I ever wrote to. Delores Macuccho, the horror author, was the second, but that was years later. That night, back in the shoebox in Texas, I slept with *Goldilocks and the Three Bears* right under my pillow. I felt I had to be its guardian since I had just betrayed it and Rosemary.

The next day I went to the library, which was not far away from home and right next door to my school. I could go there any day after school and walk home or take the late school bus home on Tuesdays and Thursdays. I often went over with Darla because they had a nice playground for the toddler group that I helped her baby-sit. Weesie was in it.

Anyway, Nancy, the librarian, asked me how I liked the book. So I told her that I loved it. I might have overdone it out of guilt for having lied about it the night before. I still remember that librarian's words. I was standing right by the gerbil cage, watching a gerbil with a bad case of eczema work out on the wheel.

"Harper," Nancy said, "if you love a book that much you should write the author and tell her."

"What?" The idea that I could actually write to an author was unbelievable to me. And what she said next was even more unimaginable.

"Yes, and often they write back. They love

getting compliments about their work just like anybody else." I guess that like a lot of other little kids I thought that authors were not quite human or alive or something. They were just names on the books. To me the books kind of magically happened. Maybe I could imagine Rosemary with her tiny paintbrush making all that fur on the bears, but did Rosemary do other things like drive a car or wash dishes? Did an author, for instance, go to the bathroom? Look, I was only seven. The thought that I could write to her and that she might write back was beyond anything in the realm of the possible. But before I knew it, Nancy was writing out an address for me.

"This is the address of the publishing company," she said. "You write to Ms. Nearing in care of them and they will send your letter on to her."

"But what do I say?"

"You just tell her you liked the book and why." Nancy tapped her cheek thoughtfully. "And you know, Harper, you look a little bit like Goldilocks." She reached across the checkout desk and tugged on my hair. I had curly, reddish-blond hair and in those days, before I grew it long, it sprung out from my head like a mess of wood shavings. "How about I take a Polaroid picture of you with this new camera the library just got?"

I blushed and rolled my eyes. But Nancy whipped out that camera fast as anything and took a picture of me looking kind of nuts and red in the face.

"Send it with your letter," Nancy said as she put the picture and the address in an envelope. I honestly didn't think that I would ever write that letter.

I might not have if it hadn't been for Nettie, a friend my mom had made at one of her prayer groups. She was a lot older than Mom. She was even a grandmother. I had heard Mom talk about her often, but never met her before that day, the same day Nancy gave me the publisher's address. I thought maybe Mom admired Nettie so much because she was older like my Gammy. But Nettie was really nothing at all like Gammy.

When I got home that day, Mom was sitting at the table with her. I knew right away she had to be Nettie. She looked over fifty, like Gammy, but much more stylish. She was wearing a nice pink outfit. Gammy always wore thin, flowery dresses that looked kind of old-fashioned. If she was slopping the pigs or working in the garden she wore old overalls that had belonged to her husband and just hitched them in the middle with a rope or any old thing. This lady wore expensive-looking eyeglasses with gold rims, and her hair looked like she'd just had it done at the beauty shop. I would bet one hundred dollars that Gammy has never even seen the inside of a beauty shop. Mom and Nettie were drinking iced tea, and Mom had made very thin lemon slices and split them over the rims of the glasses. The glasses had been frosted in the freezer, and some vanilla cookies were set out on a good plate. It was plain that Mom had gone to a lot of trouble for this lady.

"This is our other daughter, Harper, Nettie. Harper, say hello to Mrs. Peterson."

I didn't have a chance to respond before Nettie started in with "What a pretty girl you are. What lovely hair, like an angel. . . ." It's the way some adults take in a kid. It's like another kind of white noise. Not much eye contact.

Then my mother said, "Nettie is the chair-woman of our prayer groups and community affairs director for the church."

"Community communications affairs director," Nettie corrected. "That's a very important part of the job—communications. That's really what it's all about."

My mom nodded as if she understood, but I had no idea what this was all about. I thought that these grown-ups in church just went and prayed and read the Bible and maybe gabbed a little bit about whatever Bible passages they were reading. I didn't know what that had to do with community and communication affairs. It sounded like big business compared to prayer meetings. My mom was clearly impressed with Nettie and whatever it was she did.

"Where did you and Darla take the toddlers?" Mom asked.

"Oh, to the library and the playground."

Eye contact. Nettie looked hard at me. I saw my mom bite the inside of her lip.

Nettie said, interested now, "Well, did you get any books?"

"Yes," I said softly.

"Will you show them to us?" There was something very steady in her voice. I didn't like it at all.

I nodded, but I couldn't speak. And I didn't move. Then Nettie reached over and took the shopping bag I was carrying the books in right out of my hand. It was awful. But I just stood there while Nettie Peterson reached into my bag. Even my mom seemed a little surprised.

"Aha!" The sound exploded so sharply that I couldn't imagine what the cause could be. *The Three Little Pigs*? I had checked it out again, this time for Weesie. She loved the middle pig. She called him Pig-Pig, which I thought was sort of smart because he was the second pig.

"What's wrong with it?" my mom asked, tension in her voice.

"The poor wolf," moaned Nettie.

Poor wolf! This had to be a first. Who had ever felt sorry for the wolf? My mom was confused, too. "Poor wolf?" she whispered.

"Look, dear, the problem with these people is that traditional values are turned inside out. The wolf falls down the chimney and gets burned up even though he didn't hurt the pigs. He is punished for no crime. Now what kind of values are those?"

"But he wrecked their houses and scared them real bad!" I said.

Nettie didn't even listen. She was off and running. "You take a story like *Goldilocks*." My mom and I looked at each other. "Now there it is just the reverse."

"What do you mean?" Mom asked softly, her eyes still on my face.

"Well, look at the facts—Goldilocks gets off scot-free, and this is after she has trespassed, stolen the porridge, and committed vandalism. Remember?" Nettie raised a finger and began shaking it at me. "She broke Baby Bear's chair! Now you don't go around stealing and trespassing and vandalizing, do you, Harper?" She turned to Mom. "Don't we teach our children not to trespass? And not to touch other people's things?"

I was dying to remind her that she had snatched my bag from my hands and touched the books I had checked out on my own personal library card.

"So," Nettie continued, "Goldilocks trespasses and does she get punished? No. Inappropriate punishment as it is shown in these children's books is a real evil today. We cannot have stories in which naughty children get away with misbehaving. You watch it, Beth." Now she was shaking her finger at my mother. "Children start reading this trash and they get real stubborn, a lot of back talk."

"Well." My mom smiled. "Harper does like to read, but she is a very obedient child. I declare, I don't think I've ever heard Harper talk back in her life."

Nettie turned her eyes toward me. "Book-worm, are you?"

The way she said that word absolutely made my skin crawl. She made me sound like I was some spineless, mindless creature living on mold underground. I do love books, but there is nothing wormy about it. I would much prefer to be called a bat than a worm any day of the week.

Just that afternoon at the library storytime, Nancy had read a beautiful poem about a baby bat being born. It described bats' "sharp ears, their sharp teeth, their quick sharp faces." It told how they soared and looped through the night, how they listened by sending out what the poet called "shining needlepoints of sound." Bats live by hearing. I realized, standing in front of Nettie right then, that when I read I am like a bat soaring and swooping through the night, skimming across the treetops to find my way through the densest forest in the darkest night. I listen to the shining needlepoints of sound in every book I read. I am no bookworm. I am the bookbat.

I felt the envelope with the publisher's address and my picture inside my shorts pocket. It was then that I decided to write to Rosemary Nearing.

4

WITH A
LIPPITY-CLIP AND
A BLICKETY-BLICK

Nettie became a three-afternoon-a-week fixture at our table. I didn't like her one bit, but somehow I almost welcomed her. She became my challenge. She was my Brer Fox and my Brer Wolf wrapped into one, and I was Brer Rabbit. I had just started reading the stories about the funny old rabbit who lived down in Hominy Grove and always outwitted the rascals who were trying to trap him. On a tiny piece of paper I copied down my favorite part of the book. It described Brer Rabbit perfectly, and I like to think it described me. I still have the piece of paper; I keep it in my wallet. It's here with me on this bus. Here's what it says:

He was born little, so no matter whereabouts you put him, he could cut capers and play pranks. What he couldn't do with his feet he could do with his head, and when his head got him in trouble, he put his dependence back on his feet, because that's where he kept his lippity-clip and his blickety-blick.

With words like that and with friends like Gray—well, it pumps courage right into your bloodstream. But back to my story and me becoming Brer Rabbit.

I learned very quickly never to walk into the trailer with any library books on the days Nettie was around. I wasn't into open rebellion. I was eight, after all, not fourteen like I am now. I was into major sneakiness and pretending and lying.

Nettie had started to bring me what she called good Christian books with decent values. Some of the books were OK, but most of them were pretty boring, and none of them had pictures as good as Rosemary Nearing's. Everyone was happy because I was reading them all the time, but what they didn't know was that I had discovered Nutshell Library books. They were just under four inches tall and three inches wide. It was easy as pie to slip them inside the books Nettie brought over. So I learned how to sneak around and get exactly what I wanted, and everyone still thought I was perfect. I really didn't feel that God and Jesus, as much as they cared about me, gave a hoot about what I was reading. They had more important business than that to take care of.

And to tell you the truth, it wasn't just getting around Nettie that inspired me to all this sneakiness. That's just the Brer Rabbit angle. Remember the bookbat. The bookbat in me knew that my books were as important to my survival as food to eat and air to breathe. They helped me navigate. I knew I was doing the right thing. And how could I resent Nettie? Mom and Dad were so happy. I just wanted them to stay that way, and if my being sneaky helped, so what?

Mom had really spiffed herself up. She'd taken to wearing nice outfits like Nettie, when she could afford them. She stopped wearing the headband. Everyone was more cheerful, and my parents never fought anymore. Mom laughed a lot. She even laughed when I said that I thought her new fashion look was great.

The real change, though, was in my dad. He

still wasn't working at a regular job, but he wasn't drinking, either. And maybe because he wasn't drinking he kind of found his tongue and discovered he had a way with words. It was as if a new Hank Jessup had suddenly been born, but not exactly born again. This was more of a personality rebirth than a spiritual one. And it all seemed to happen in one night. It was the same night I found out what they had really been up to at all those meetings at the church.

I had been baby-sitting Weesie, who was being a royal pain. In desperation, I was about to call Darla next door when Weesie finally conked out. I had just gotten into bed myself when I heard all this loud talk outside. Clear as anything I heard Nettie, who has a tight little voice that sounds sort of like stitches ripping.

"Well, Hank, Beth has a fellow she can be right proud of in you. I thought I might split when those TV people showed up and started asking you all those questions. I mean, I had contacted them but I didn't think they'd really come. Sakes, you sure did pull it off."

My parents, Nettie, and at least four other people came into the trailer, excited as a bunch of little kids and talking a mile a minute. They would show those so-and-sos a thing or two about these New York smut peddlers. There was no way their children were going to be exposed to aliens.

I thought I must have heard them wrong. If I hadn't, this was about the most exciting thing to ever come to the Melrose Glen Trailer Court. I lay very still in bed pretending to be asleep. Never in my eight years had I thought that I might have a chance to meet up with an alien. The idea was enough to keep me wide awake for hours. I had a little E.T. figure, and it was the cutest thing.

I listened hard for more talk of aliens, but there wasn't any. But there was plenty of talk about another word that I didn't understand at all: "humanism." I knew we were humans, but this new word confused me totally. I had heard my parents use it often lately. As I lay in bed pretending to sleep, it was practically dripping off everyone's lips.

"It's here, humanism, right here in our school district." Nettie's voice was ripping away.

"You see, my problem," said a man whose voice was very thoughtful and slow, "is that I see this as a violation of our rights as parents. That was what was so good about what Hank said to the TV lady who came over to the church tonight. What we are teaching here at home and church is being undermined."

"It's a Satanic attack on the American home," Nettie said.

"You're right, of course, Nettie." I recognized my dad's voice. "But we can't use that kind of talk on television. It just makes these folks think we're crazy."

Slow Voice spoke. "Hank's right, Nettie. They love to point a finger and say we're ignorant bigots."

Dad continued. "In truth, it is a situation of parents with traditional Christian values wanting to be responsible for their kids' upbringing and not turning the children over to a bunch of government hirelings."

"We know what is best for our children." Mom's voice was strong, with a quiver of passion. "I know what is best for my daughters. No government is going to love my daughters the way I love them."

Silence fell. My mom's words had really done something, like she had struck a deep truth. My mom had just said that she loved me more than the United States government ever could. I felt very safe and very secure.

I was the only one in the shoebox that did. These grown-ups had more fears and worries than you could shake a stick at. My dad had said not to mention Satan on TV, but that didn't mean they shut up about him that night. Satan, the elitists, and the humanists, like a gang of spiritual outlaws, were at large and about to invade every school and home in America. And in our trailer was a meeting of the posse getting ready to ride out after them.

I soon learned that this gathering was a follow-up to the first official meeting of F.A.C.E., or Family Action for Christian Education. The Monday night prayer group had changed to Tuesday night, and it was no longer a prayer group. They did a little bit of praying, I guess, and a whole lot of talking.

Their first act had been to have Nettie, in her role as communications director, call up a local television station and invite a reporter to come to their meeting. Their next act, that night in our trailer, was to start making up a list of how children were harmed by books. There were books that showed people being threatened, books that specialized in what they called bedtime terror, books that included May ham. I didn't understand that last one at all. I thought maybe it had something to do with Easter, when we often had a ham dinner. And Easter happens in the spring, though around April, I thought, not May, but one never knew. There were books on their list that were just too sad, like one about a girl named Anne Frank. It was a chapter book, I thought. I had just started to read chapter books that year, so I decided I might try it. How could it ever make me sad? After all, my mom had just said she loved me more than the United States government ever could.

I realized as I heard them making the list that my reading days were numbered. And I didn't quite know what to do. Should I stop reading for the sake of my mom? She was right that nobody would ever love me and Weesie as much as she did. But I just couldn't believe that these awful things they were saying would ever happen to me. I had read a lot of those scary bedtime books. Sometimes I got scared, but when Mom would come in to kiss me good night I would smell the vanilla on her fingers and the monsters just shriveled up. And what if Rosemary ever answered my letter? I could never write back again if I was never allowed to read another one of her books. I began to feel very sorry for myself.

Then I remembered my old friend. *Born little . . . he could cut capers and play pranks*—Brer Rabbit! What would Brer Rabbit do? Would he whimper around, sniveling and being scared? Not that smart rabbit. He would figure out how to do the reading, never get hurt, and never let on. He'd fool Satan. He'd fool nervous parents and all the rest of those Christian worrywarts in F.A.C.E. And guess what ol' Brer Rabbit would become? The best Christian of the whole lot.

And guess what else? It worked. It worked for almost five years. Not only that, the very next day I received an answer from Rosemary Nearing. So I just think it was meant to be.

5

WENDY, GAMMY, AND THE MAGIC PEBBLE

The new Hank Jessup, the one who had been speaking so impressively while sitting at our kitchen table the night before, was suddenly not just at the kitchen table. I heard the same voice early the next morning saying almost the exact same things. "It is really just a situation of parents with traditional Christian values wanting to be responsible for their kids' upbringing and not turning the children over to a bunch of government hirelings."

Something in the sound of his voice was a little different. I got up and wandered out to the kitchen area. And there were my dad and mom silently drinking coffee, and up on the television screen in living color was the new Hank Jessup being interviewed by KETX's Eileen Briggs. She was really pretty, with chunky gold earrings, a suit with sharp white lapels, and a hairdo that glistened like a golden helmet. This lady could have been a White House reporter. But there she was in front of the Melrose Glen Missionary Church, holding that mike up to my dad.

At this point I would like to say, "The rest is history, dear reader." I just love the way those old-time authors like Mr. Dickens or George Eliot (who was actually a woman, in case you didn't know) stop smack-dab in the middle of the story and say stuff like, "patient reader," and then give some little side comment. It's so cozy. But there is no room for coziness here, and to stop and tell you that the rest is history leaves out half the story. Let's just say: so began the next significant chapter of Hank Jessup's life. And mine.

The phone started ringing like crazy that morning. When I came home from school it was still ringing. Darla was there answering it. I walked in just as she was patiently explaining that Mr. Jessup couldn't be on the *Paul Fletcher Fireside Chat* show that night because he was already scheduled for *Lone Star Nightly News*, but if she could take the number, either he or Mrs. Jessup would call back.

Darla held Weesie in one arm, and with the phone tucked between her shoulder and ear, she motioned to the kitchen table. There was an envelope, a beautiful envelope with my name written in the most magnificent swirling letters. It was addressed to:

> Ms. Harper Jessup
> 64 Melrose Glen Trailer Court
> Melrose Glen, Texas 76203

Around the edges of the envelope were intertwining vines, leaves, and flowers drawn in ink. There were even birds calling my name. In the upper corner of the envelope, opposite the stamp, was the return address: R. Nearing, Cider Mill Road, Dorset, Vermont 05251. My heart was thumping hard. Rosemary Nearing was real. She lived on a road with the wonderful name of Cider Mill in a real state with a real zip code. She probably did go to the bathroom.

I took the letter back to my bed. I wanted to read it in private. It took me at least five minutes to open the envelope because I was scared to death of wrecking one of those beautiful flowers or tearing off the wing of a bird. When I finally got it open, out dropped a picture of Rosemary. She was sitting on a stone wall holding a cat and she had this huge mass of blondish-gray hair foaming around her face. It was as if she were looking directly at me. She had a regular, friendly face, yet right away I noticed that her eyes were different. You just knew that they saw more than other eyes. They could pick out hidden colors, and they could see the shine in an animal's eye or how the wind turned a leaf.

Here's what she said:

Dear Harper:

What a special thing it is to receive a letter from someone who has read my books and enjoyed the illustrations as much as you seemed to. You notice all the little things that I worry people will miss.

To answer your questions: I make the animal fur bristly by first using a rapidograph extra-fine tipped pen. I thin out the ink wash (Winsor Newton permanent black) 40%. Have you learned percentages yet? Ask your mom or your dad or your teacher. For the sky

I use a very mild bleach solution over that to get that nighttime milkiness of moonlight. Making the porridge was the easiest part of all. I just used plain old watercolors and made up about eight different shades of gray, then fiddled with it.

Thank you for your picture. I think your librarian is wrong. You don't look anything like my Goldilocks. You have a lot more character. Possibly a Wendy, as in P. Pan.

Your friend,
Rosemary Nearing

Possibly a Wendy! I sank back on my bed. Could life get much better?

Actually, life did get better. From the time Rosemary Nearing's letter came and my dad first appeared on the television news, everything started to change.

Sometime in the next twenty-four hours my dad got a chance to replace an air conditioning duct in the church, but that was the last chore he ever did in jeans for the Melrose Glen Missionary Church. He didn't even put up the drywall in the new F.A.C.E. office the church set up in the basement, next to the reception room. Somebody else did that. He was downtown with Nettie and Mom buying a new suit, as well as new shirts because white doesn't look so good on television. He had to get light blue.

Over the next few weeks we hardly saw him. He was in the newspaper four different times, and I cut the pictures out to put in my scrapbook. He looked so handsome. He had a new haircut that cropped off all his curls, but it did make him look more businesslike. And, as Mom said, it emphasized his deep-set eyes. His long, thin face had filled out. He looked more serious than ever, but not sad like before. Boy, *did* he look serious, like a president of something or an executive. Mom showed me pictures and quotes of things he had said that were published in some religious magazines and newsletters. F.A.C.E. was starting up its own newsletter. Dad was going to be the publisher, Mr. Slow Voice was the editor, and Mom and Nettie were going to be something, too. The church was going to pay for them to take typing lessons or learn how to use a computer or something.

One year later, just after I turned nine years old, the change was more than blue shirts or a new haircut for my dad. This was really big. The trailer rolled. Not far, but it still rolled, right into the church parking lot. We were allowed to hook up to church power. No more noisy generator. There was a playground right there and, best of all, the library was even closer than before. As far as I was concerned, life was great. My parents were happy. My dad looked handsome as all get out. My mom looked sensational in her new clothes and she still smelled like vanilla.

Even Nettie was fine. For my ninth birthday she bought me an outfit that was a lot like one of my mom's that Nettie and Mom had picked out together. Of course, she would have taken it right back to the store if she had known what book I was reading. I had just finished reading a whole mess of chapter books and I was longing for a picture book for a change. So when I went to the library one afternoon, I was intending to get another Rosemary Nearing picture book or maybe a slew of those little Nutshell Library books and just read them on the spot.

When I walked into the library, I saw this big poster from a picture book with some nutty-looking donkeys on the cover. But it wasn't the book cover that got me. It was the black-and-white photograph of the guy who wrote the book. I stopped dead in my tracks.

"What is it, Harper?" Nancy said.

"Put a wig on that guy and he looks exactly like my grandma!"

She laughed.

"I'm serious. Gammy looks just like him. And she's very pretty," I added quickly. "And he doesn't look like a girl. It's so funny."

I read his book called *Sylvester and the Magic Pebble*. It is one of those books, the best kind, that makes you happy and a little bit sad at the same time. A donkey named Sylvester finds a magic pebble. If he holds the pebble, he can make any wish he wants and it comes true. Then a lion comes along, and poor old Sylvester panics and he says, "I wish I were a rock." You guessed it, he turns into a rock. That's why this guy, Mr. Steig, is such a good writer. He makes Sylvester do just what any kid would do if he saw a lion: panic. Sylvester can't get *un*rocked because you have to touch the pebble for the wish to work. His parents are so sad. Sylvester's mom is just like my mom; she loves him more than the United States government could ever love him. One day his parents go out for a picnic and come right to the Sylvester-rock, where his dad finds the pebble. Sylvester can hear them and is wishing he could be with them, and the moment his dad puts the pebble on the rock—bingo, their beloved son is back.

I just loved that story, and so did Weesie when I read it to her. But I knew that I could not bring it home because magic was on the list. Not only that, turning a donkey into a rock might count as an animal mutilation. I had finally found out what May ham meant. It didn't have anything to do with Easter. The word was mayhem. Mayhem was listed right before monsters and dragons on the harm list, which I had sneaked a good look at in the F.A.C.E. office. The list said, "mayhem (persons and animals having parts cut off or bitten off/torture)." Guess what was at the top of the mayhem list—the Brer Rabbit Stories. Brer Rabbit sometimes resorted to mayhem, I admit. Once he tricked Brer Wolf and locked him in a trunk, drilled holes in it, and poured in scalding water. Of course, Brer Wolf had run off with Brer Rabbit's babies and eaten several of them. My mom would have done the same to anybody who had eaten me or Weesie.

Even though I couldn't bring *Sylvester* home,

I just had to share how much I liked the book with somebody other than Weesie. And I thought of Gammy. I had to tell her she looked just like this guy who wrote the book and drew the pictures. She is the kind of person who would think that was interesting. So I wrote her a letter.

Three weeks later, right before Halloween, a big box addressed to me and Weesie arrived from Gammy. You won't believe what was in it. Two donkey suits and two magic pebbles! Gammy had made them herself out of fake fur and had sewn ears and tails on them. They were the cutest things you ever saw.

But there was one hitch, and it was a big one. Nettie was there just when Weesie and I were tearing open the box.

"What!" Nettie squeaked at my mom. "Surely you're not going to let them celebrate that pagan holiday." I looked up at Mom and saw her eyes grow dark and troubled.

"Well, Nettie," she said. "It's not as if they were dressing up as witches or ghosts."

My mind was working fast as anything. Lippity-clip, blickety-blick, that old rabbit was back, ready to outfox that silly Nettie.

"Well, now," I said, slow as syrup in best Brer Rabbit style. "I just remembered something, Mom."

"What's that, darling?"

"I just remembered that in Sunday School Reverend Abbott said that for the Christmas pageant they would like to have Joseph come in leading a donkey with Mary riding it, but that last year that old donkey they had went to the bathroom on the stage. Now I could be the donkey in this suit, and I know that I'm big enough to carry Mary because it's Betty Sue Gilbert, and she's barely bigger than Weesie. And I won't go to the bathroom on the stage."

Mom and Nettie laughed their heads off at that one, and Nettie said, "You are the cleverest little thing." Mom told me, as soon as Nettie left, that she would certainly let me and Weesie try out the donkey suits on Halloween night. I made Weesie promise to hush about the magic pebbles we would take along.

Tell me, was this not a prank worthy of Brer Rabbit himself? That December I even carried the magic pebble right through the whole Christmas play, wobbling across the stage on all fours while I carried Betty Sue Gilbert to Bethlehem.

6

GRAND DELUXE BLASPHEMY

Our trailer had been hooked up at the church for more than a year when Reverend Abbott came over one night to tell us the bad news. There was talk about zoning ordinances and city sanitation codes, and the bottom line was that we would have to move back to the Melrose Glen Trailer Court. I remember my mom sighing and saying, "Well, it could have been worse. It could have happened right before Christmas."

But then, like magic, out of the bad news came good news. At least I thought of it as good back then.

The very next evening Dad came rushing into the trailer.

"We're not going back to the trailer court."

"What?" my mom asked. She stopped rolling out the cookie dough. "Did Reverend Abbott fix things downtown?"

"No, honey. I fixed things."

"You mean we get to stay?" I asked excitedly.

"No, Harper." He leaned over and put his hands on my shoulders. "We're going to become missionaries."

"In Africa?" I asked.

"No, don't be crazy. Think I'm going to take my wife and babies and plunk them down in the middle of a foreign continent? No, honey bunch. We're going to Durmond, Oklahoma, where they're teaching blasphemy in the schools."

Mom had two smudges of white flour on her cheek. "The schoolbook thing?" she asked.

"The schoolbook protest, honey. We got the money."

"From F.I.S.T.? Oh, Hank!"

"Reverend LePage called me himself."

"He didn't!"

"He did, and guess what else?"

"What?"

"We're getting a brand-new Roadmaster Grand Deluxe motor home."

"What?" Mom jumped up into Dad's arms and wrapped her legs around his middle and they started dancing around the shoebox. Then Weesie got all excited and began hopping around holding onto their knees. So I just piled into the jumping heap. We were actually going to roll, and roll in a Roadmaster Grand Deluxe. I had heard people talk about them over in Melrose Glen Trailer Court. Darla had an uncle who had actually owned one. She said it was the prettiest thing you ever saw, and as long as a city block.

When everything had calmed down I thought, *Goodness, blasphemy might be bad but it sure has brought us a lot of good.* I wondered what kind of blasphemy they were teaching over in Durmond, Oklahoma. So I asked.

"Evolution." My father spat the word out.

"What's that?"

Mom and Dad looked at each other sort of funny. Then my mom said "Well, Harper, you know how in the Bible, in Genesis, it says that God created the earth in six days and on the seventh He rested?"

"Yeah, so?"

"Well." She took a deep breath. "There are some very mixed-up people out there."

"Very dangerous people," my father said in a low voice.

"What do you mean?" I asked.

"They believe that it didn't happen that way." Mom took the Bible off the shelf, opened it to the book of Genesis, and began reading in that soft voice of hers. "In the beginning God created the heaven and the earth. And the earth was without form, and void. . . ." She skipped to the verse that said, "So God created man in his own image" and stopped reading just before the part about resting on the seventh day because Weesie began to whine.

"You explain the rest, Hank," Mom said over her shoulder as she picked up Weesie to take her to bed.

"It's very simple," Dad said. "They flat out are calling this book a book of lies and God a liar."

"How do they do that?" I asked.

"They say it didn't happen in seven days but millions and millions of years. And they say that God didn't make man but that man was born from an ape."

"What?" My jaw dropped. I thought that Dad and Mom and Nettie might have been a little too nervous about stuff like Halloween and some of the books they objected to, but this was different. The whole idea was just plain ridiculous.

"Dad, that evolution idea is the stupidest thing I ever heard. Are you sure that's what they really say?"

"I'm sure, Harper, and you got to be careful when you're around these types. They try to sneak their ideas into your head. Your brain must become a fortress against these ideas; your heart must be an arsenal—an arsenal for our Lord Jesus Christ who was not, I repeat, *not* a monkey!" He did have a way with words, my dad.

I was still trying to figure out how anyone could come up with such a harebrained notion as this one. "But Dad, even if they were right . . ."

My dad cut me off sharply. "What do you mean, even if they were right? They aren't." He eyed me as if a few bricks in the fortress of my brain might be coming loose.

"Don't worry. I told you, I know it's the stupidest idea I ever heard. I'm just saying that even if they think they are right, how come there are still some apes around, in Africa, for instance, and in zoos and stuff?" Dad was looking hard at me now, and Mom had just come back from putting Weesie down. "I mean it just wouldn't be fair, and God is fair."

"What do you mean, Harper?" Mom asked.

"I mean that if it were true that people were once monkeys or apes it would be very cruel of God to let some stay monkeys and others, you know, go on and be people. And I really believe that God just loves every creature for what it is and wouldn't want to go improving some and not others." What I was really thinking was that it seemed terribly unfair that a monkey would never have the chance to live in a Roadmaster Grand Deluxe motor home.

Mom and Dad just stared at me. Then Mom swallowed and hugged me tight. "Harper, I declare, you are the sweetest and the smartest child in the whole wide world."

And Dad said, "Beth, I couldn't have put it better myself. Harper, I think you're going to have to start going on talk shows with me."

"Oh, no!" I said quickly. "I couldn't ever be on TV or the radio. I get stage fright. I nearly died being a donkey in the Christmas play at church, and nobody could even see who I was in that outfit." Mom and Dad laughed hard at that, and they both hugged me again. I knew that I really could never go on TV—what if the librarian saw me bad-mouthing books with my dad? Worse than that, what if Rosemary Nearing saw me— me, the possibly Wendy girl?

After I went to bed, Mom came in to kiss me good night again. She was carrying the Bible and sat down on the edge of the bed.

"Thought I'd read to you a little bit. The creation story is so beautiful."

"Sure," I said. "You still got flour on your cheek, Mom." She tried to rub it off but it wouldn't come. "Here, let me lick it off." I pulled her toward me until her hair flopped over onto my pillow. I took a big lick all the way up her cheek and we giggled.

"You're some nut, Harper," Mom said, smiling, and she opened the Bible.

"In the beginning God created the heaven and the earth. And the earth was without form, and void; and darkness was upon the face of the deep. And the Spirit of God moved upon the face of the waters."

I tried to imagine the darkness of the void as I snuggled down farther under the covers. As Mom read on, I remember thinking that six days did seem like an awfully short time. Maybe time was different way back then. I snuggled closer to my mom, my nose grazing the gilt edges of the book's pages. The smell of vanilla crept over the words.

7

ROADMASTER TO NARNIA

It all happened so fast. Within two weeks we had our new Roadmaster Grand Deluxe and were on the road—me, Weesie, Mom, Dad, and Wingo, the newest member of our family. The Roadmaster was so big that Mom had said we could finally have a small pet. Fish wouldn't work because the water would slop out of the bowl when we were on the road, and we were going to be on the road a lot. Mom had suggested a gerbil or a hamster, but I saw enough of those in the library. I had a hankering for a bright green parakeet. I talked Weesie into it, which wasn't hard. She was just five years old. We hung Wingo's cage in a space behind the dining alcove.

The Roadmaster was so luxurious. There was wall-to-wall carpeting everyplace but the kitchen and the bathroom. Mom had specified the avocado color scheme for all the kitchen appliances (even a dishwasher), and the carpet was green, too—so Wingo fit right in. I had a great room all to myself. No more sharing with Weesie. There was a closet and a little hinged desktop that folded down from the wall. It was like a little office of my own.

The most exciting discovery of all happened just as we pulled into Durmond, Oklahoma. We had stopped for lunch and Mom and Dad had taken Weesie to the McDonald's playground for a little exercise. I was rummaging around in my closet, where I had dropped a necklace Nettie had given me as a good-bye present. Under my hand, the floor of the closet moved a little. Then I noticed a very small keyhole and a raised edge along the closet wall. I pulled at the edge with my fingers and part of the closet floor came up on hinges. On the bottom of the panel I had lifted was taped a small key. I had discovered a hidden compartment.

This is just like the first book of the Chronicles of Narnia, I thought, *like that gray drizzly day when*

Lucy walks into the wardrobe and all the coats and the walls melt away to become a beautiful, magical land. Then it dawned on me. *Wait a second, Harper! You have your own secret hiding place here*. I had had to leave the second book of the Narnia Chronicles back in Melrose Glen half read. I had never even dared to bring it home for fear my folks would find it, and it was the hardest book to stop reading. But with a secret compartment like this, there would be no stopping. It would be easy to hide any book I brought home. Several books! I couldn't wait to find the library in Durmond. I reached inside the roomy space and explored every dark, wonderful corner. I felt just like Lucy, who one moment had been rubbing her face against old winter coats and the next was in an enchanted forest in the snowy night. It didn't matter that I was actually crouched in a Roadmaster parked at McDonald's in Durmond, Oklahoma. The thrum of the highway faded as this precious doorway opened up. Never again would I have to leave books behind.

As excited as I was about the secret cubby, I soon learned that my parents were not even very concerned about library books anymore. Their new thing was school textbooks, particularly science ones, and this effort didn't disturb me much. I was a little nervous about going into a new class in the middle of the year, but it turned out that the fifth grade in Oakdale Elementary was not much different from the one in Melrose Glen. The desks were arranged in almost the same U-shaped pattern. Instead of an aquarium, Oakdale had a terrarium with some lizards and stuff in it. The best thing about the school was that it only went through sixth grade, which meant you didn't have to bother with big kids. That was sort of a relief.

There was a pretty girl named Wendy in my class. I hoped that she would be my friend, and I tried to tell her how Rosemary Nearing had said I was possibly a Wendy. But the whole story died on my lips when we were out on the playground. She looked bored when I started to talk to her and then she and a few other girls ran off to the jungle gym. They didn't exactly invite me to come and I'm not the pushy type, so there I was standing alone on the playground. I went over to the chain-link fence and pretended to examine it. Stupid, huh? Right. Like I'm some sort of fence expert. Ever try to look busy when you're alone in some public place where everyone has a friend or a job to do? You don't look busy, you just look dumb.

On the other side of the fence, I saw a guy spraying the grass with a hose attached to a bag on his back. I sort of wished I were him. He looked so relaxed. Of course, there are risks to all those chemicals. He might get cancer. I thought about that, which led into one of my favorite games, called Would You Rather. I got the idea from a book that gave funny but impossible choices like would you rather have your mom make a scene in a restaurant or be eaten by a hippopotamus? Here was my fifth-grade version of Would You Rather: Would you rather stand alone on a playground feeling dumb or look busy by spraying pretty green grass with something that might give you cancer?

I didn't stay at Oakdale Elementary long enough for the choice to become a real issue. We were there a couple of months, three at the most, just long enough for Mom and Dad to get the ball rolling. The ball was evolution. Dad had been reading all this stuff that talked about how Genesis wasn't just a Bible story but actually had a lot of scientific facts to back it up. He said it could be scientifically proven that God had created all things and creatures in six separate days and that there was definitely no monkey business. He and Mom tried to get their point of view represented in the classroom, but the school wouldn't let Dad come in to teach. Then my parents asked if I could be excused from the classroom during science. That didn't work, thank goodness. Even though I hadn't made any friends, I didn't want to appear any weirder. And then before I knew it we were gone from Durmond. On the road again.

As far as my dad was concerned, Durmond had been a lost cause. I heard him on the phone to Reverend LePage. "You got to give me back-up, Dan. There was no one in that community who wanted to join in. This is all about community values, but the church there just wasn't organized enough to get the folks fired up. . . . Yeah, you're right, we need some good groundwork done before we move in. OK, Garland, Nebraska, it is then. But Durmond was a washout."

That was Dad's view. Durmond was not a lost cause for me, however. It was in Durmond that I made the wonderful discovery of inter-library loan, the greatest invention since the light bulb. I had just finished *The Magician's Nephew* and I wanted to read the next book in the Narnia series. I worried that maybe the library in Garland wouldn't have it. But then Phyllis, the librarian in Durmond, told me about interlibrary loan. If the Garland Library didn't have a book they could call Durmond, and if Durmond had it Phyllis would send it right out to Garland for me. All the libraries were linked together, so no matter where I moved, as long as I had a library card I would be part of a web as powerful and beautiful as the one in *Charlotte's Web*. Just as Charlotte the spider wrote messages in her web that transformed Wilbur the ordinary pig into "some pig," this web would transform me. I would eventually collect nearly fifty different library cards. I was snagged forever in the wonderful web of the public library system.

8

THE BOOKBAT'S
FIRST AXIOM

We were in Garland, Nebraska, for only a few months. Other families joined the blasphemy battle right away. This time I did get taken out of class during science, and I liked the fact that I wasn't the only one. There were four other kids: Emmaline, Jenny, Roberta, and Jerry. Emmaline was memorable because, although she was just a fifth grader, she was "developing," as they say. I think that made my mom nervous. She would say things to me like "That Emmaline is certainly mature-looking. I hope she doesn't give you any funny ideas." I had no idea what Mom was talking about. But the fact was that we five kids were thrown together quite a bit because our parents were all part of the Community Values Group, a local group connected with F.A.C.E.

I got used to coming home and finding all the moms meeting in the Roadmaster. As the weather turned warmer, they would sit in lawn chairs under the retractable awning drinking iced tea and planning strategy. In the evenings there would often be a meeting at one of the houses, and the men would come, too. One of their plans was for the women to go out door-to-door during the day and get people within the school district to sign a petition. I found out about this the hard way.

I was in the school library with my class one day, during a choice period that we had on Fridays. I was sitting on the floor where the nature books were, in the 500s, and I was looking at a beautiful book on birds. It had incredible photographs that showed the barbules of a feather, which are fringy things on the edges of birds' feathers. Magnified a hundred times or more, the feather looked like a magical forest. The word "dinosaur" caught my eye. "The oldest bird is said to be archaeopteryx. This strange creature, with its pigeon-sized teeth, feathers, and wishbone, is thought to be the link between modern birds and dinosaurs. Other small carnivorous dinosaurs are also possible ancestors of birds. If one carefully studies birds today, one can find many anatomical features that link them with dinosaurs."

Well, knock my socks off! I thought. On the next page there were some amazing drawings that compared the anatomy of birds and dinosaurs. And, bingo, there was Wingo! There was a photograph of an ordinary modern-day parakeet, though blue, not green, and next to it was a tiny reconstructed dinosaur's head that had been found in Colorado. The bones came together in a shape that looked a heck of a lot like Wingo's little head and beak. It was pretty exciting to think of Wingo as a dinosaur, which made a lot more sense to me than all this talk about people and monkeys and the book of Genesis.

I was sitting there imagining Wingo as a dinosaur when suddenly I heard voices whispering nearby. It sounded like the school librarian and one of the second-grade teachers.

"No—oh, Doris—these people. I can't believe it!" the librarian said.

"I'm not kidding."

"You mean they walked right up to the front door and said 'Do you want dirty books taught to your child?' "

"Yes, and what's a person to say—oh, by all means, I want dirty books taught to my child." I felt something inside me begin to crumble. The librarian said, "This is so scary."

"It is. And, you know, they're very organized."

"That's even scarier."

"Whose class is the Jessup girl in?"

"Harper? She's in Mrs. Barren's. And she's a voracious reader."

What was I supposed to do now? I stayed quiet so I wouldn't get caught. Knowing that I'd been eavesdropping was bad enough, but what was worse was that I had a sudden vision of my mom and I hated it. I knew she got together with these people and had meetings all the time, and that was why Emmaline, Jerry, Jenny, Roberta, and I were always being thrown together. And because they were so organized we were going someplace new the week after school ended. Jerry's parents were filing a suit against the school board for their right not to use the science book and something to do with equal time. Roberta's father was running for the school board. I had thought that the lawsuits were the big strategy. I hadn't realized that part of it was my mom going door-to-door asking people if they wanted their children to be taught dirty things from dirty books. I turned back to the page with the picture of the feathery magical woods and thought of Wingo as a dinosaur. For the life of me I couldn't figure out what was dirty about the whole idea, but I knew they were talking about books like this one. It didn't matter whether this book was a textbook or a plain old regular library book. They would hate it either way.

I felt worse now, hearing this stuff about my mom, than I ever had. And I felt powerless, the way I sometimes do when I hear bad stories on the news, like those reports about starving children or hundreds of people being massacred. Powerless and defeated.

I realized then a very weird but simple truth: although books were as much a part of my life as anything had ever been, as much a part of me as the air I breathe or the blood that runs through my veins, nothing I had ever read in a book had in itself caused me to be really, truly unhappy. Real low-down, rank, grotty unhappiness does not come from books. It comes from life. Now that I've had some geometry I know the word "axiom"—it describes something so obvious you almost don't notice it, the way all three angles of an equilateral triangle are equal. So now I call this truth The Bookbat's First Axiom. But I probably just called it a rule back then, although I kind of hate to think of a truth as being a rule.

9

GAMMY AND
THE MOON LADY

After Garland there was Lincoln and Omaha and
Wichita, and then bunches of teeny tiny towns
like Twin Lakes and Clydesville and Goshen and
Kokomo all through the Midwest and the South.
They had little school districts that were poor and
couldn't fight any kind of organized effort. And
F.A.C.E. was organized.

At the end of the summer, right before I went
into sixth grade, we made a quick detour to Georgia to visit Gammy. Weesie and I were so excited.
It had been a long time since we had seen Gammy,
but I had dim memories of her house. Even after
the glories of the Roadmaster I was anxious to
get there. Gammy's house didn't have an indoor
bathroom. I liked that. You had to walk up to

the johnny house, which was kind of an adventure. I think Mom was a little bit embarrassed about it, though. Gammy joked once that the reason Mom had moved down to town and stayed with a girlfriend for her last two years of high school was for the plumbing more than the convenience of being closer to school.

The most fun, though, was that Gammy said that I was old enough that year to sleep in the loft, which was a cozy little space up under the beams of the house in the living room. I would sleep on a mattress under one of Gammy's beautiful patchwork quilts.

Gammy never seemed much older, just softer and whiter, powdery white, with hair as snowy as the goose down that poked through her pillows. She kept geese and chickens and one cow that she taught Weesie and me to milk on that short visit. Gammy said my mom had been a great milker, which was hard for me to believe. Mom seemed so different from any little girl who would have grown up here, johnny house or not. And she sure was different from Gammy. They hardly even seemed related. Maybe Mom was more like her father. But he had died before I was born, so it was hard to figure.

Gammy had a garden patch strung with sweet

peas and beans. The pumpkins, even in August, swelled like big orange moons in the red Georgia dirt. We walked out there, me and Gammy, on our last evening in Blue Hollow. Gammy was chuckling and carrying a pitcher of milk.

"Don't tell me, child, that you've never seen anyone sop a pumpkin?"

"No, ma'am."

"Well, I never thought it was such a secret, thought everyone knew that if you want a big ol' pumpkin you gotta feed it. And here's how you do it." She squatted down by one of the smaller pumpkins. "OK, you little runt," she said cheerfully to the pumpkin. "You want to catch up with your brothers and sisters?" Then she laughed and looked up at me with her sharp blue eyes. "I never really thought about that before."

"What, Gammy?"

"Sex and pumpkins."

I stared at her. My parents never ever said the word, and here Gammy had just let it trip off her lips as if it were nothing.

"Wh—what about sex and pumpkins?" I whispered.

"I was just thinking that there must be a male and a female, and I wondered how you'd tell the difference between the brother pumpkins and the sister pumpkins." She was busy with a small paring knife. "Here, see what I do. I make a notch in the vine right here, low to the ground. Then I take this wick from the kerosene lamp—got to be sure to use a clean one—and just put one end in the pan." She poured some of the milk from the pitcher into a shallow pie tin. "Now that wick will just sop up the milk and the pumpkin will drink it. See, I put the pan a little higher than the notch to make it easy for the pumpkin. They just love milk, pumpkins do. Don't you?" She patted its orange sides.

Gammy knew all sorts of stuff like this—sopping pumpkins, putting mud on bee stings and cobwebs on nasty scrapes. She knew how to call down an owl and how to deliver a calf even when it was coming out upside down and crosswise. She knew that when smoke hugged the ground it would rain within the day and that if hickory nuts had a thick shell a hard winter was coming. She knew more ghost stories than you could shake a stick at—spirit stories, she called them. And it was spirit stories that got us in trouble.

As we walked back to the cabin, the moon was already up, sailing over the points of the pine trees.

"Why, mercy, Harper!" she exclaimed. I just

loved the way she said my name. It came out "Hopper"—very soft, like the breeze blowing through the trees. She stopped short in front of a puddle. "Look at that old moon dancing in the puddle." I looked down and saw a perfect reflection of the full moon shimmering in the water.

"Well, I think we got to call down the moon tonight."

"How do you do that?" I asked. Gammy had so many exciting ideas. She was as thin as a rake, but really strong. Her pale rose-colored dress blew around her scrawny ankles and the tops of her work boots. She reminded me of one of those creatures who, despite their fragility and small size, could defy gravity—like an insect that could walk up a wall, or a butterfly that could fly thousands of miles over mountain ranges and deserts.

Gammy poured a little splash of milk into the puddle and the milk swirled into the moon's reflection. Then she looked straight up at the moon and began to sing in her soft voice,

> Moon lady, silver gal,
> Sailing through the night,
> Here's some milk from our pail.
> Here's our earth's delight.

Come, come, come on down,
In your silver rain.
Come, come, come on down,
Make our lives less plain.

"That ought to do it," Gammy said. "Now the moon spirit stories will come to me."

"Flat-out blasphemy!" The voice ripped through the air, shattering the peace of the evening. My father raced out from behind the woodshed and dropped his kindling on the spot. "You will not be telling my daughter these heathen lies."

I had never been so afraid of my father in my life. His face was twisted into an ugly mask, and the moonlight gave it a sickly sheen. I could hear short gasps from Gammy. I was so scared for her I forgot to be scared for myself, but I felt paralyzed. I wanted to reach for Gammy's hand just to hold on to her. I was afraid she might have a heart attack or something and just slip away from me, slip away as the moon was doing behind a cloud racing across the sky. Then I heard Gammy catch her breath and swallow.

"Henry," she said in a very calm voice, "these are just silly old stories that people have been telling around this hollow for years, our local Blue Hollow stories. They're not even scary ones, these Moon Lady tales."

"It doesn't matter, Lou. You're not telling them to my daughters and that is that. We are Christians."

"So am I, Henry. And don't you forget that the first things your wife ever learned about the love of God she learned from me and her father."

"Listen," my dad hissed. I couldn't believe what I was seeing. My father took a step closer to Gammy, raised a finger, and shook it not more than an inch from her nose. "We're the parents. We do the raising here, and we don't want any interference. Not from you, not from the government, not from those left-wing types—nobody."

Well, I just about died on the spot. I hated my father. I reached over for Gammy's hand, but it wasn't there. I slid my eyes over to her. She had put down the milk pitcher, and her thin arms were folded firmly across her narrow chest. Her mouth was set and I could see a pulse beating in her wrinkled neck.

"You listen to me, Henry. I am seventy years old and nobody—not you, not the government, not these left-wing commies you're talking about, not the President of the United States, not even our Lord Jesus Christ—comes up to a seventy-year-old lady and shakes their finger in her face." And with that Gammy picked up the pitcher and stomped back to the cabin. Like a fly on a wall, like a butterfly scraping across a headwind, that was Gammy.

We were gone before the moon started to climb down the other side of the night. I cried. I cried all the way out of Georgia and into Tennessee. Mom sort of sniffled. She thought Dad had been a little harsh, but she couldn't believe that Gammy had said that thing about Jesus not shaking his finger at her. So she thought it was best for us to leave. She said she planned to write Gammy a long letter explaining how we all loved her but how she and Dad knew what was best for their children.

I thought the real question was not whether we loved Gammy, but whether Gammy could ever love us again. I was almost eleven and beginning to realize how truly weird and unlovable my family seemed. Not to mention flat-out rude. I hoped Gammy wouldn't blame that on Weesie and me.

10

Are You
There, Judy?
It's Me, Harper

We got a new Roadmaster, even longer than the first one. It had a deep freeze, so we could have ice cream a lot, and a microwave. There was an even bigger Narnia cubby in the floor of my closet. Everything should have seemed better.

But it wasn't. I kept thinking about Gammy. I wanted to write her but I was embarrassed. Every day it became harder and harder to write and easier and easier not to write. Finally I just gave up, but I felt crummy about it.

That fall we were in two different schools in Tennessee. The communities were pretty well organized. Now the focus of F.A.C.E. wasn't so much on the science books as it was on this new reading series that had just come out. It showed women driving trucks and men cooking; F.A.C.E. thought this would screw up role models for us. Actually, Dad often made Weesie and me grilled cheese sandwiches on the weekends when Mom was at the Laundromat, so I didn't get what the problem was.

That first week of school, Mom and Dad kept asking me what we were reading and told me to look out for this stuff with boys in the kitchen and girls with trucks. I hadn't seen any of that in the books so far, but I let it slip that we had read this story called "A Visit to Mars." It was OK, but not nearly as good as *The Martian Chronicles*, which I had found in the library that summer.

The school wouldn't let you bring these reading books home, so my mom went to school and read the story and found something worse than girls with trucks: thought transference. I thought it was pretty cool myself—conversations formed in the characters' brains without anybody talking to each other. Mom and another lady from the local organization of F.A.C.E. thought this was confusing. It was confusing to Lorraine, the other lady's daughter, because she hadn't read as much science fiction as I had. But I knew that this kind of thing happened in books all the time.

It was the same old story. Soon me and

Lorraine and two other girls were excused from class during reading to go to the library, as our parents requested. Actually, it was great fun. We were supposed to be reading another, more old-fashioned reader, but we never did. We talked mostly about girl stuff. Lorraine and Debbie had already gotten their periods, but Mandy and I hadn't. Lorraine and Debbie wore bras. Mandy sneaked an old one from her older sister and sometimes wore it. Debbie generously offered to give me a training bra of hers. I just knew that I could never ask my mom to get me one. My mom hated talking about this kind of stuff; she had kittens anytime I mentioned anything about periods, bras, or whatever. She and Nettie had been on a radio show back in Melrose Glen once, and Mom had said that parents should teach their children about sex rather than leaving it to the schools. I think she really thought it should be left to God, but God was not going to take me to the mall and buy me a bra. When Mandy got her period, I was the last one left. I felt totally freaky.

Now I will never be sure if this is exactly how it happened, but I think that Mrs. Carroll, the school librarian, might have left the book out on purpose. Mrs. Carroll let us gab away in the library all we wanted and never checked up on whether we were reading the old-fashioned readers. Sometimes she brought cookies for us. No wonder we loved going there during reading period. Anyway, I suspect that Mrs. Carroll overheard us talking about periods or something, because *Are You There, God? It's Me, Margaret* seemed to mysteriously pop up. It was great.

This was not a possibly Wendy situation. Judy Blume, the author, made Margaret Simon exactly like me—a late developer. Margaret was the last one in her group of friends to get her period and all she and her friends did was think about bras and sanitary napkins and boys, just like Mandy, Debbie, Lorraine, and me. Judy Blume is some writer. She described what it was like when this one girl's period starts exactly the way Mandy described it. She put in all the excitement and wonder that a girl feels when it first happens. And Judy Blume must be used to getting her period because from the picture on the book jacket she looks to be at least thirty-five. So that's what I call good writing.

We all read the book at least twice. Sometimes when we were in the library, while the other kids were reading the series our parents hated, we would read aloud from the Margaret book. Those kids in the classroom could have the martians; we would take Margaret any day of the week. Mrs. Carroll never objected. She just sat behind her desk fixing up torn book jackets and helping the little kids make their selections.

It was Mandy who got the idea that we should have a secret club like Margaret and her friends. So we started thinking up names. Margaret and her friends had called their club the Pre-Teen Sensations, or the PTSs. It was a good name, but we didn't want to copy.

"I don't want anything with the words values or family in it," Mandy huffed. "I'm just sick and tired of F.A.C.E. and the community values stuff."

"Yeah, this club is about us, not values or families," said Lorraine. I couldn't have agreed more.

We tried hard to stay away from the word teen or pre-teen, but kept coming back to it. "Well," I suggested. "We are almost adolescents. I think I read that technically adolescence begins when you're thirteen."

"I'll be twelve next month," Lorraine said.

"Well, heck," said Debbie. "What are we

going to call ourselves, the Almost Adolescents? AA, like Alcoholics Anonymous? That won't do."

Something dawned on me. "I got it! We're not almost adolescents; we're pre-adolescents."

"So?" Mandy said.

"Well, I was reading a lot of medieval stuff last summer and they often call young ladies in those books maidens or damsels." I paused for dramatic effect. "We could become the Pre-adolescent Damsels, or the P.A.D.s."

Well, they all hooted at that one, and I saw Mrs. Carroll's shoulders shaking as she hurried into her workroom.

When we stopped laughing, Debbie said, "Harper, you're too much. Calling ourselves P.A.D.s! Yuck!" We all started giggling again.

"Wait! Wait! I've got it, another one," I said, raising a finger. "Why are we all here?"

"Because our parents don't like that reading series with the men cooking and the martians doing the mental thing," Mandy answered.

"Precisely!" I said. "The martians—that's why we're here. We ought to call ourselves the Martian Maidens."

Mandy's eyes brightened. "How about the Mental Martian Maidens?"

"Oooh, great!" Lorraine and Debbie cooed.

"Yes, definitely," I said. "And we can call ourselves the Three M's."

Everybody loved that.

But I had to leave town before our first official meeting. We had planned to go to the mall, where Debbie and Lorraine and Mandy were going to chip in and buy me a box of Personally Yours sanitary napkins so I would be ready when I finally *got it!* It was a very Judy Blumish thing to do. I'll tell you, the Mental Martian Maidens were the three best girlfriends I ever had, even though I knew them for less than six weeks. I missed them something fierce. And what would I do when I finally did get my period? Mom was so weird about all this. I was feeling so alone. I kept thinking, wondering . . . are you really there, Margaret? Are you there, Judy? It's me, Harper.

11

HOTLINE
TO HEAVEN

It was right after the first of the year and we had left Tennessee. We were heading west again to a whole bunch of poor school systems out in Arkansas. We had stopped for the night near Little Rock, and I had taken Weesie to the playground. It turned real cold all of a sudden, so we came back to the Roadmaster before long. As soon as we stepped inside, I knew something was up. There was a little zing of tension in the air. Mom and Dad were kind of dressed up, and Mom was wearing big pearl earrings and some eyeshadow. A man I didn't recognize was sitting at the table; his back was to us as we stopped just inside the door.

"Beth—I may call you that, mayn't I?"

"Oh, certainly, Reverend LePage."

"When I go into my chapel, Beth, and have my morning chats with our Father and tell him of your and Hank's efforts, he's listening. He says to me, 'Dan, these are your missionaries. These are the good Christians who will help make the people understand the devil in those pages.' And I listen to him. I know his plans for you."

I had never heard of anyone having such close contact with God. This man didn't have just the Lord's private phone number, but his appointment book, too. He talked on about God's agenda, as he called it. It was as if God had let him, Dan LePage, take a peek over his shoulder.

It seemed to me that God's agenda sounded a lot like Dan's. And Mom and Dad were going along with it! Maybe it shouldn't have surprised me. If this was God's agenda, and if Dan's agenda agreed with God's, well, there must be a Roadmaster there somewhere. So how could my parents not believe this guy? It kind of scared me. I wasn't quite sure why. But I'll say one thing, that voice of Dan LePage drove me nuts. It was soft, too soft. My sensors went up, the same way Brer Rabbit's did when Brer Wolf or Brer Fox was laying a trap.

When Reverend LePage paused, Dad said, "Here're the girls." The man came right over to us, picked Weesie up, and started carrying on about what a pretty little thing she was. She was, too. Same color hair as me but soft and straight, bright blue eyes, and no freckles. But Weesie was almost seven and I really felt that: a) she was too big to be picked up as if she were some little toddler, and b) it was kind of rude.

The reverend looked at me with not nearly so friendly an expression and said, "Now, how old are you, young lady?" I didn't answer. I hate people who call girls "young ladies." Makes me feel like a miniature feminine thing, all proper and fussy. Stupid. I just hate it. But the very worst thing is that it puts a girl in her place. Even though, you see, unlike Weesie, I was too big to pick up, I felt like I had been whittled down to size anyway.

Reverend LePage was the man behind F.I.S.T., Families Involved in Saving Traditional Values. They left off the V because it was neater that way. I had heard my parents talk of F.I.S.T. and Reverend LePage often; it was F.I.S.T. that was funding F.A.C.E., so people like Mom and Dad could go out and do their missionary work.

It was F.I.S.T. that had bought us the Road-master Deluxe. You would have thought the Queen of England had come to visit. My parents had an almost giddy look about them. My mom had no need for the pink blusher on her cheeks because she already had the bright spots she always gets when she's excited.

"How old are these lovely young ladies?" Reverend LePage asked, setting Weesie back down.

"Louisa is almost seven and Harper is eleven," Mom said.

"Oh," he said shortly, giving me a quick look. "She"—he paused—"is reaching that troublesome age. A lot of guidance required. We're very firm, my wife, Patty, and I."

I couldn't bear this creep. "You know," he continued, "these hormonal things start twitching." I turned beet red, but my mother turned redder. I thought she might start twitching herself.

"Well, I think it's time for them to get ready for bed," Mom said.

Was she nuts? It was only five-thirty. But she couldn't say homework because we were between schools. Weesie and I went back to our rooms. I could still hear Dad and it made me cringe.

"Well, Dan, I can't tell you how gratifying this has been to me and Beth, your support and all. The new Roadmaster is a superb piece of machinery, I'll tell you."

"You're going to need it, for you'll really be putting on the miles in the next few months. But it's working, Hank, it's working. We're getting the word out. We've got challenges to instruction in thirty-seven states now. And we're spreading it out to all aspects of the school curriculum. It's sex education, it's history, it's science, it's literature with the foul language and this new surge in the teaching of witchcraft. We got 'em. If they can teach Satan's religion, we can teach ours—equal time. The alarm has gone out and people are responding, Hank. They are responding because of the hard, in-the-trenches work of people like you and Beth and, God bless 'em, even those darlin' little girls of yours."

Oh, don't bless me, God. Don't you dare bless this young lady!

Dan LePage was definitely real life, and he made me feel that kind of low-down, grotty sadness with all this young lady stuff and the rest of it. So I thought about my Narnia cubby. I had long ago finished reading the Narnia series, and by now I had discovered this guy, Lloyd

Alexander, who wrote about the kingdom of Prydain—a place full of magic, battles between good and evil, terrible enchantresses, and good princesses. I had his book *The Black Cauldron* in the cubby, and I had the precious Margaret book in there. I had actually bought it at the mall with some money I had saved from my allowance.

But oh, Lloyd! Oh, Judy, it's me, Harper, again. There's this guy here with a hotline to heaven. I'm getting kind of desperate.

12

CUSTER'S A CREEP AND I WANT NYLONS

That was not the last we saw of Reverend Dan LePage. He would occasionally drop in on us wherever we were. In the spring we all went to the annual F.I.S.T. conference in Denver. There were picnics and barbecues; we got to go gold panning in a creek outside Denver and there was a rodeo. Lots of neat stuff for the kids.

But I was mad at Mom because whenever we went to the conference services and everyone dressed up, I was still wearing stupid white ankle socks while other girls my age were wearing nylons. I couldn't believe it. I would be twelve in a few months, and although I still hadn't gotten my period, I didn't see why I should be doomed to wearing white socks. Forget the training bra! One did not have to be a mental giant to see that the chances of my talking my mom into buying me one of those were zero. I could hardly concentrate on singing, my favorite part of church, because all I could think about was the fact I was wearing an undershirt and ankle socks.

From Denver we went up into South Dakota. They weren't so organized as in other places—there were a lot of Indians and what my dad called a dangerous liberal element in the region where we were. They needed a lot of help getting the local F.A.C.E. group going. Good library, though. I got on my western books kick. And for the first time in my life I really let my guard down.

We were sitting around the table in the Roadmaster and my dad was talking about going to some state park on the weekend. He had heard it had a historical museum about the Black Hills. I wasn't too keen on all this touristy history, but my dad was just the opposite. We'd already gone to Mount Rushmore, which I admit was totally cool, but when Dad said Reverend LePage's profile should be right up there with Tom Jefferson, George Washington, and the rest of them I nearly barfed. Mom, of course, agreed with Dad.

My dad kept talking about how this area was a country made by real heroes with "man-sized Christian dreams." He and Mom had periodically talked about retiring here. They loved the broad plains and the immense dome of the sky. It was pretty neat, but I didn't see a lot of man-sized Christian dreams. We had spent some time up near a reservation and I had just seen a lot of very poor Indians. So there we were sitting around the table and Dad is talking again about the glories of this country. I had just finished reading a book about how the white people had ripped off the Indians in the war for the Black Hills, which were the Indians' sacred ground. And my father actually said that Reverend LePage was a "latter-day Custer." I had only been half listening; most of the time these days I was worrying about getting my period, or figuring out how to get Mom to let me wear nylons. But when Dad said this I guess I looked pretty shocked.

"What are you looking so surprised about, Harper?" Dad asked.

I blurted it out. "Custer was a total creep."

"Why, for goodness sakes," Mom said. "Custer was a hero. Where'd you ever get an idea like that?"

"A book." As soon as I said it, I knew there would be trouble.

"What book?" My father leaned forward.

Lippity-clip, blickety-blick, my mind was racing. This was a trap, but I had accidentally set it up myself. What would that old rabbit do? If I told them that it was a library book, which was the truth, then I risked not being allowed to go to a library ever again. If I told them that it was a history book, not only was that a lie but I might have to show them which book so they could go after it and put it on the list. It took me about two seconds to decide what to do.

"It was a history book."

"Which one?"

"Oh, I don't know, maybe back in Arkansas. Or it might have been Tennessee. I'm not sure."

"Well, what did it say?" My father pressed.

"Oh, just that he was a . . . a jerk."

"It said he was a jerk?" My mom's mouth dropped wide open.

"No, no, it didn't use that word," I stammered.

"But you interpreted it that way, didn't you? Admit it, Harper." My dad sounded impatient.

I knew I was in trouble. Where was that rabbit when I needed him?

"You made an interpretation. You see, Beth, this is just what Dan LePage is talking about—at this age Satan can make inroads into a young mind."

"Reverend LePage knows nothing about me or my mind." My voice had risen and there was a lump swelling in my throat.

"You hush up!" My father pointed a finger at me just the way he had at Gammy that night she had tried to sing down the moon.

"I am not making interpretations about Custer being a jerk. He was. There are facts."

Mom was swallowing hard and fingering the edge of her sweater. "Well, well, now, dear, why don't you just tell us some of these facts." She was trying to smooth things over, trying to get me off the interpretation hook, but the way she said "these facts" made it sound like they weren't facts at all.

"To start with, he was really stupid. He graduated at the bottom of his class at West Point. Nearly got kicked out."

"A lot of people couldn't even get into West Point. So I don't think that it's so stupid to be at the bottom of the heap," my dad said.

"He wasn't a real general."

"What do you mean, he wasn't a real general?"

"He was a brevet general."

"Isn't it the same thing?" Mom asked.

"No. It's like being a substitute, a temporary general. But he got himself all gussied up with the stars of a general—that's against the rules. And he was very vain. He dyed his hair and wore perfume."

"He did not!" My father spat out. "Next thing you're going to be telling me is that he was a homo."

"Hank!" my mom exclaimed.

"He invaded the sacred land of the Sioux, the Black Hills. He broke the treaty. He said he was doing it for research but it was just for gold, and that started the whole mess."

"Those are heathen lands and they cannot be called sacred."

"It doesn't matter. The government made a treaty with them, heathen or not."

My dad threw up his hands. "You see, Beth, you see what they're teaching them in these public schools—total and complete disregard for heroes, for authority figures—anti-God, anti-authority, anti-everything."

"Anti-Indians," I said quietly.

"What?" my dad barked.

"Nothing!" I screamed, and ran out of the Roadmaster.

There was nowhere to go. We were parked at an RV place on the edge of this nothing town. The plains stretched like an endless pale brown cloth to the rim of a cloudless sky. I had on new running shoes that Mom had bought me, so I just took off. I ran and I ran and I ran. The ground turned hard and cracked. I jumped over a deep gorge and half hoped I wouldn't make it to the other side. I scuttled down a sandy slope. I was crying, my nose was running, and my lungs hurt so bad that it practically killed me to take a deep breath. My pink-and-white running shoes had mud all over them.

I ended up at a place where the land dropped right off. It felt like the edge of the world. And I had such rage in me I just had to get rid of it. One of those hot, dry, prairie winds came up and slammed me right in the face. I opened my mouth as wide as I could and screamed, "Damn you to hell, Custer!"

I didn't come back for an hour or more. When I was finally about a half mile from home I saw my mom running like a crazy woman. Her hair was flying around like streaks of lightning.

"Mom!" I called. I had to shout it again because the wind had really come up. Finally she heard and began running toward me in a funny, lopsided way. The heel of her shoe had broken off and her face was wet with tears.

"Oh, Harper!" She was gasping my name over and over again. "Harper, darling." We collapsed into each other's arms. I was sobbing.

"I didn't mean to be bad. I didn't mean to. I'm not a bad girl, Mom, I'm not."

I couldn't believe I was saying it, but it felt good. I hoped Brer Rabbit wasn't watching. The more I said I was bad, the more Mom told me how good I was.

"Come on, darling, it will all be OK. You know your dad gets overheated sometimes. We'll clean you up. You look a fright. You need to wash your face."

I stopped right there and looked at her. "Mom, I need a sanitary napkin."

She looked straight back. Her eyes were mournful. "OK," she said quietly.

I had felt it just the way Judy Blume described it, right after I screamed at Custer. I was so thankful. I had been twelve for almost two months. I couldn't face seventh grade without my period. Mom got me the napkins, the training bra, and nylons all in one trip to the mall. I guess she just gave up. At least that was what I saw in her eyes—those sad, sad eyes.

13

ScF Edd
Plus ScF Mac
Equals Gray

Before I knew it I was an eighth-grader. We were in Spoonwood, California, and were going to stay for a while. School would start in six weeks, and there was actually the possibility that I might spend my entire eighth-grade year in one school and then even stay for high school. Mom had been pressing for this ever since the blowout in South Dakota. She thought that maybe I needed to be a little more settled, and with high school approaching she knew it would be harder and harder to keep moving around. Dad didn't mind the idea. He was getting a little tired of being on the move and said that maybe now would be the time to make his break into the policy and administration area of F.A.C.E.

F.A.C.E had been growing by leaps and bounds. They no longer were so financially dependent on F.I.S.T. and were thinking of opening up major headquarters in California. There was talk of F.A.C.E and F.I.S.T. together buying some cable stations, which would be a dream come true for my dad. Many a night I heard him and Mom talking. "I see this thing going right to the top—the sky's the limit, Beth. I think we've been about as effective as we can be in these field operations. The next logical step is television."

It sounded fine to me. Maybe Mom was right—we needed to be settled for a while. I hadn't had any real problems keeping up in school, but math was getting harder because if you missed something in one town and the next town was ahead it was difficult to catch up. I couldn't imagine being able to do that kind of catching up with algebra, which was just around the corner. Although one good thing about moving around was that I had a great collection of schoolbook covers. I'd started covering my library books with the paper covers the schools gave us to protect our textbooks. That way I could read anytime and Mom and Dad thought I was doing my homework. Yet I was starting to realize that the moving also meant that my closest friendships were with librarians and gerbils. I had never found anybody quite like the Mental Martian Maidens back in Tennessee. I had started to miss them again more than ever.

It seemed like we got over what happened that afternoon in South Dakota, at least on the surface. But Mom never quite lost that sad look in her eyes, and I started to worry about it more and more. I knew that we had come to a major fork in the road out there and it had a lot to do with the fact that I was growing up and changing. I mean, I wanted to grow up really bad. I guess that's natural. But when I was sobbing about being bad, that was something else. I guess I was trying to stay little and precious for my mom because that made everything easier for everybody.

I wanted things to be easy. I didn't want to go back to when Dad was drinking and we lived in that crummy shoebox of a trailer with the white noise of the generator going all the time. It had been almost six years since Mom's tooth got broken in the fight, but I had never forgotten getting down on the floor and looking for those little pieces. Since then Mom had gotten her tooth capped, and I had become a master of diverting, ducking, bobbing, weaving, and lying. Now I had created my own generator noise by proclaiming myself a naughty child. It was not a trick worthy of Brer Rabbit. For the first time I really felt ashamed. I couldn't cover the truth forever. But I didn't know how to stop.

I loved Spoonwood as soon as we drove into it. The campground where we parked the Roadmaster was in a grove of live oaks on the edge of the city limits. It was a really pretty town, and so small that you could walk almost everywhere. There was an elementary school that went through sixth grade and a junior high that went through eighth. For high school the kids took a bus two miles away to the next town over. I would be able to walk Weesie to school every morning and then be at my school in another two blocks. The public library was right next to the junior high. I hoped that we would stay in Spoonwood a long, long time.

We had driven right by the library on our way in and it looked like they were having a summer bedtime story program. I saw kids wearing pajamas and holding teddy bears. Once we got the Roadmaster parked, I convinced Mom to let me take Weesie over. Weesie was eight-and-a-half and could be really stubborn. I thought that it looked like fun. She thought it was babyish.

"Come on," I urged her. "I saw an ice-cream truck pulled up."

"You did?"

"Yeah." It had been a long hot drive from Bakersfield.

"I think it looks babyish to be wearing your pajamas and everything."

"It's not babyish. It's kind of teenage. It's like a slumber party."

Weesie's eyes brightened. I had said to Mom earlier that if we stayed here awhile and I made friends I wanted to have a slumber party in the Roadmaster. Mom said there might not be enough room, but that maybe if the kids had tents we could work something out.

"Will you wear your pajamas?"

"Me?" I said. I remembered I had heard my dad say something to Mom about how Dan LePage might drop by that evening because he was over in Dalton, just ten miles away. "Sure," I said quickly. I would do anything to avoid Dan LePage—even wear pajamas to the library.

So that is how I met Gray Willette on my

very first day in Spoonwood, California—standing in my pajamas holding a teddy bear in the stacks of the Spoonwood Public Library. The little kids were downstairs listening to the librarian read a story and having milk and cookies. Weesie had handed me her teddy bear to hold while she had the snack. I had wandered off to the fantasy section of the children's room but realized I had read just about everything there. So I asked another librarian if there was a new Lloyd Alexander book or anything. Everything he suggested I had read.

"Well, it sounds as if you've read through everything down here. Time for you to go upstairs." He pointed. "Go up the stairs over there, then through the double red doors, turn right, and the fantasy section is against the far wall, directly beneath the windows."

I went upstairs and started browsing. Almost immediately my attention was drawn to the title *Queen of Sorcery*. I was in ScF Edd, and this book was by David Eddings. The spine said the book was the second in the Belgariad series. I pulled the book out, stuck Weesie's teddy under my arm, and started reading. I was hooked right away.

There was going to be a problem, however, that I had not anticipated. Adult novels are usually larger than kids' novels. This book didn't fit into the Lincoln City Bullfrogs book cover I had brought. There was no way that I could just tuck this book bare under my pajamas, go home with it, and sneak it into the Narnia cubby. And, believe me, this was a book that would really upset my parents. I had been planning to get library cards for Weesie and me, so I guessed I could check the book out and ask the librarian to keep it for me. I could think of some excuse—but what? This librarian didn't know me yet. I didn't want to come right out and tell him that my parents were weird about books. Definitely a problem. I thought I would just read a little bit more and then figure out what to do. So I sat right down on the floor.

"You planning on sleeping here?"

I looked up and saw a kid about my age wearing a black T-shirt printed with orbiting planets and stars and on it the words "We have loved the stars too fondly to be fearful of the night." He had sharp blue eyes, standout freckles, and red hair. Georgia-dirt red hair, I remember thinking, and that reminded me of Gammy.

I had put Gammy out of my mind for months, as far back as the blowout in South Dakota. That day I had cheated Brer Rabbit and I'd cheated Gammy. But when I looked up at this kid, even though I should have been embarrassed that I was dressed in my pajamas and had a teddy bear jammed under my arm, I felt good. The cheating was over. I don't know whether it was just the color of his hair or what that made me think of Georgia, but it was as if I had let Gammy back in my life and maybe I could let this person in, too, whoever he was.

So right there I said, "I know this sounds strange, but I have a favor to ask." I guess it did sound strange, because he looked a little bit startled.

"Uh, sure."

So I just said it. "Please, can you keep this book for me after I check it out? I have this problem with my parents, and I can't sneak it in tonight to this little cubby where I keep stuff that might upset them."

"Cubby?" he asked. His eyes widened a little and lost their sharpness.

"Yeah, well, see, we live in a motor home and back in the closet across from my bed there is a hidden cubby in the floor. I call it the Narnia cubby."

"Oh!" His eyes sparkled now. "Kind of like the closet that Lucy went through."

"Exactly," I said excitedly. I couldn't believe it. It wasn't just that he knew about Narnia. I could tell that he knew what I meant by a Narnia cubby. It was all there in his eyes. He knew that I didn't actually think I was Lucy going through a real door to magical lands. He knew that the cubby in the Roadmaster was a sane person's ticket to freedom of thought. And I felt in my bones that Gray was a bookbat like me—one of those creatures that hums through the night; one who sounds out the darkness with "shining needlepoints."

Even if he wasn't a bookbat, Gray was still far from an undernourished reader. So he didn't think I was weird when I asked him to help me. And he did help me. He took the book, gave me his phone number, and told me I could come over and read it at his house whenever I wanted.

"What are you reading?" I asked as we walked to the checkout desk.

"*Vampire Fetus.*" I must have gulped. "Yeah, it is a kind of shocking title. But don't let it put you off." He held the book up. It had a stunning jacket with a little red blob floating around against a purplish background; within the blob were two fuzzy points that looked like baby fangs. "Startling but tastefully done, I think," Gray said. "None of this comic-book superhero graphics stuff. Haven't you ever read Delores Macuccho?"

"No, never even heard of her."

Gray stopped dead in his tracks. He looked at me squarely. "Delores Macuccho is the foremost craftsperson of the horror novel. She is the most direct inheritor of the Edgar Allan Poe tradition."

"I guess I better read her. I kind of like Edgar Allan Poe. Is she anything like Stephen King? I like him, too."

Gray looked horrified. "Stephen King!" There was a long pause. "I don't even mention him in the same breath as Delores."

I liked this guy. I smiled and stuffed Weesie's teddy bear under my other arm. "You call her Delores?"

"We're sort of on a first name basis. We write."

"You do?"

"Well, once. I wrote her and she answered. She called me Gray. So I feel I can call her Delores now."

"I once wrote an author."

"Who?"

I felt a little embarrassed, but then I caught myself. Once long ago I had betrayed Rosemary by pretending that the Goldilocks book I had loved wasn't really that good. I wouldn't do it again.

"Rosemary Nearing." I said her name firmly.

"Oh, yeah, I know her. She's cool. I liked her stuff when I was little."

"So you think I should start reading Delores Macuccho?"

"Definitely."

"What should I start with?"

"The Witch's Therapist."

"I think you better keep that one at your house, too."

That was the beginning of my friendship with Gray Willette.

14

A LIGHT
AND AIRY PLACE

But books were not to be the main problem in Spoonwood. Just when you finally have the game down pat, they change the rules on you. It took me a while to catch on to the new program.

When Weesie and I got back from the library, Dan LePage was there talking to my parents. He couldn't pick Weesie up anymore; she was too big. Instead he just said, "Hello, girls. Let's give the old reverend a kiss." He crouched down and stuck out his cheek.

Weesie ran right over and planted one on him. I would rather be dead. I had to think fast. I decided I couldn't exactly say, "Sorry, old reverend, but I've got a sexually transmissible disease." Instant cardiac arrest and we would have three dead Christians on the floor of the Roadmaster. Instead I looked at my mother and said, "I've got a terrible canker sore. I don't think anyone should kiss me."

"Oh," Reverend LePage said quickly. It almost sounded like a cough, and was probably his shortest reply ever.

I went straight to bed. I could hear the adults talking, but I blocked it out, as I did most things my parents discussed with Dan LePage. If I had listened, I would have clued into the changes in the rules; I would have realized that it was a whole different game that had the worst implications for Weesie. I did learn soon after we came to Spoonwood that the heat was off the books, off the curriculum, off what the schools were teaching. I thought that my life would be easier. How wrong I was! But I was so happy with my first impression of Spoonwood that maybe nothing would have penetrated even if I had been listening. That night, I could hardly wait for morning so I could call my new friend Gray.

The phone rang four times before I heard a click and a recorded voice that sounded like Gray's.

"Hi! You have reached the Elvis-sighting hotline. If you wish up-to-the-minute information on Elvis sightings in the continental United States, press one now; for sightings in the polar regions, press two now; for Elvis sightings in McDonald's or another major fast-food franchise, press three; for sightings in Laundromats, press four. If you have a rotary dial phone or need additional help, stay on the line and one of our operators will be happy to assist you. If you are calling for Gray Willette, he is mowing the lawn. Leave a message at the sound of the tone."

"Uh, hi. This is Harper Jessup, the girl you met in the library. I mean the girl Gray met, not Elvis." I started giggling so hard that I had to hang up and call back when I caught my breath. Gray called about an hour later. He invited me to come over and to bring a bathing suit for the swimming pool. I had never met anybody who had a pool. I thought it was pretty exciting. Weesie was going to something with Mom at the new church we would be going to in the next town over, so I was on my own.

I should have known that nothing Gray Willette ever did was quite normal. The answering machine was a tip-off. When I got to his house, I went around to the back as he'd told me to, past a greenhouse attached to the house, and through a little gate. There was a swimming pool, but from where I was it seemed to be empty. I walked closer and saw that there was all of eighteen inches of water in the bottom; Gray, wearing a sun hat and sunglasses, was floating around in an inner tube with *Vampire Fetus* propped on his knees. He glanced up and must have guessed what I was thinking.

"Well, there is a drought in California, you know. They've got an ordinance saying you can't sprinkle lawns or fill swimming pools."

"Oh," I said.

"But it's still cool on a day like this. Your book's over there on the table. Did you bring your suit?"

"Yeah, I just wore it under my clothes."

"Well, come on in—there's another tube over by the tree."

For a fleeting moment I wasn't sure if there would be enough water for the two of us. I know a thing or two about Archimedes' law, the one about a body in water displacing its weight in liquid, and I thought there was just a slight possibility that when I got in the pool Gray and I might end up on the bottom. But nothing happened. We just floated around drinking soda, eating chips, and reading. I can't think of a better way to spend a day when it's 102 degrees.

When our toes began to shrivel, we went inside. Gray's bedroom had posters all over and a computer that he said his grandparents had bought for him. And there was a gerbil in a cage.

"Oh," I said. "This gerbil has a bad case of eczema."

"I know. We've tried a lot of stuff but none of it works, or it will work for a while then the eczema just gets bad again."

"Have you tried Triploz?"

"No, what's that?"

"It's for baby eczema—you know, human babies. But it works for gerbils. If you mix some Brylcream with the Triploz when the fur starts coming back, it makes the fur softer, so it's not all bristly."

"How do you know so much about gerbils?"

"I just do, one of those things you pick up from traveling around the country a lot and hanging out in libraries."

"Jeez, maybe you could become a gerbil veterinarian."

"I don't think there's a whole lot of money in it."

Gray laughed. I could tell that Gray himself

was a very funny guy, so if I could make him laugh I thought that was pretty good. "What's your gerbil's name?" I asked.

"Jane Fonda."

"Jane Fonda—like the actress?"

"Yeah, except we named her for the aerobics, not the acting. Jane the gerbil really loves to work out, in spite of her chronic skin condition. When my mom does the Jane Fonda exercise tape, this little Jane goes crazy. We bring her out where the VCR is. They work out together."

"They do?"

"Yep, the fur might be flying but she's pumping—pumping fur, I guess." We both laughed hard at this. "You see," Gray said as he took Jane out of her cage. "She could become a little poster gerbil—inspiring other rodents despite her handicap."

"I don't think eczema would really count as a handicap."

"It's all relative. For a gerbil this might be pretty bad. Jane is physically challenged." Gray grinned and raised an eyebrow. "That's the politically correct way of saying it."

"What do you mean, 'politically correct'?"

"You know, the right way to say or act so you don't offend a minority. Like my mom—she works for the telephone company. She climbs the poles when they're doing installations. They used to call them all, male or female, linemen. Now they call them linepersons. Mom says she doesn't care what they call her as long as she gets the same pay and the same benefits. She's not that politically correct, or p.c., as they say."

"My parents aren't either, I guess."

"Well, people go into overdrive about all this p.c. stuff. I'm not sure it really adds up to much."

"What does your dad do?"

"He's a swimming pool salesman, but business is tough right now, so he's also taking some computer courses at the community college."

I took the gerbil from Gray and looked at her. "You're right about Jane, I think. We might be talking about a real handicap here. This is the worst case of eczema I have seen since . . . since Box Elder, South Dakota."

"Maybe we should get some of that stuff you were talking about."

So we walked into town and picked up a tube of Triploz and some Brylcream at the drugstore. When we got back we could hear music from inside as we came up the walk to the front door. Gray's mother was home.

Mrs. Willette waved to us with one of her

hand weights as she pounded her way through the exercise video. There was Jane the gerbil in her cage, set on the coffee table, running like crazy around on the wheel and up and down the ladders. Mrs. Willette pointed to the gerbil and laughed, but she never missed a beat. She was beautiful. She had red hair, freckles, and the same bright blue eyes as Gray. Her face was really merry-looking, and she had dimples that punctuated all her nice expressions.

"Time for the cool down," Mrs. Willette said to Jane. But Jane just kept going until the end of the tape. When it was finished I put the ointment on all her bald patches.

Mrs. Willette was one of those people who made you feel instantly at home, like she was genuinely interested in you. The problem was that I suddenly clammed up. It dawned on me as we were sitting there, Mrs. Willette drinking her cool-down beer and Gray and I drinking grape soda, that this was the first family that I had met for years that wasn't connected with F.A.C.E or F.I.S.T. The Willettes were a family that I had met on my own.

It was hard to explain to Mrs. Willette what my parents' job was and why we were always moving around. I mumbled something about my dad working for a church organization; Mrs. Willette—Colleen—didn't press me. We mostly talked about school. Chances were that Gray and I would wind up in the same eighth-grade class.

I was a little bit sad to leave the Willettes' house that afternoon. It was so spacious and airy, with its windows looking out on the lawn and the dining room that opened into the greenhouse full of sprouting seedlings and hanging plants. For the first time I thought of the Roadmaster as a shoebox. It seemed so narrow and dark compared to the Willettes' house. And it was hard to imagine my family with a gerbil named Jane Fonda or a mom who spent the day climbing telephone poles. This was a very different family from any I had ever met.

15

DELORES, MERLIN, SATAN, AND BARBIE

When I got back to the Roadmaster, a family very much like those I was used to was there. Mom and Weesie were visiting with a lady named Gina Allman and her daughter, Cindy, who was Weesie's age. Gina was the head of a local group called United Christian Mothers. The Allmans would be taking over the schoolbook protest. I guess I should have been happy that it wouldn't be us anymore. My mom was giving Gina a tour of the Roadmaster because the Allmans would be getting one soon and setting off on the road at the end of the school year. Weesie and Cindy had become fast friends, which was good because Weesie would have a friend for the next seven or eight months and would be less dependent on me. But Gina Allman made me nervous, the way that Nettie used to. She was so bossy and sure of herself. She had this insistent tone that crept into everything she said. Very know-it-all.

"Don't go to the Clip 'N' Curl in Spoonwood," Gina was saying as I came in. "The owner's a homo and they've got new hairdressers in there every week, a lot from San Francisco, and that's the AIDS capital of the world." I was tempted to tell Gina that I had never heard of contracting AIDS through getting a haircut or having your hair colored.

When Gina and Cindy left, I told Mom that I thought Mrs. Allman was kind of bossy.

"Oh, Harper, you judge too quickly. She's a well-meaning person."

"She's the one who's judging, and I don't think she's well-meaning at all. All she did was bad-mouth people."

"Oh, Harper, don't get so excited." That sad look crept into her eyes. "And please," she said, "just hush about your feelings on all this when Dad comes home." I looked into the dark flickering of those sad eyes and I think I began to get the first glimmerings of what was to come. This was not just about values but about me and Mom and Dad. It was a triangle, and Mom felt caught between us.

But I put it out of my mind. For I, too, had made a new friend, and it seemed that the Willettes wouldn't mind if I was over there all the time. They lived close enough for me to walk so I didn't have to depend on my folks to get me over there. I didn't hurry up and tell my parents that my new friend was a boy. They would have gotten nervous, even though Gray and I were not romantic by any stretch of the imagination. Mostly we would just float around in the pool, reading and eating. Jane Fonda's eczema started to go away, and within three weeks the fur was coming back. Mrs. Willette thought I was a genius. And I thought Mrs. Willette was the most beautiful, strong lady I had ever met.

The first time I saw her in action on a telephone pole was just after my dad bought a car. Mom and I were driving over to the approved beauty shop in the next town for haircuts. We stopped at a red light, and when I glanced out the window, there was Colleen getting ready to climb a pole, her red ponytail sticking out from under her hard hat, and cable and tools hanging off her belt. It was all I could do to keep my mouth shut and just watch, but I knew I couldn't risk Mom's reaction. She'd think climbing poles was a pretty weird job for a mother. So I quietly watched Colleen climb straight up that pole, fast and powerful and very graceful, as though it were the most natural thing in the world. Who would ever want to be a gerbil veterinarian if you could do something like that?

On our way back from getting haircuts we stopped at the Allmans' to pick up Weesie.

"Want a cup of coffee, Beth?" Mrs. Allman asked. She turned to me and said, "The girls are in the rec room playing with their Barbies." Great! I thought. Just what I always wanted to do.

Cindy had a Barbie house, Barbie Cadillac, and just about every piece of Barbie equipment imaginable.

"You take that Barbie over there, Weesie," she said, pointing to one on the floor by a pile of doll clothes.

"I don't want that one. Her hair's knotted."

"She's fine. Don't be silly."

"But you always get to play with the pretty one with the pretty hair, and I'm the guest."

"Shut up!" Cindy said.

Gads, this kid was a pain. I couldn't for the life of me see why Weesie put up with her. The girls proceeded to play dolls the way little girls always do: walking them around on the carpet, getting them dressed and undressed, moving them through the scenes of life.

"OK, we're going to church. Ken can be the minister. . . . doo da doo da doo." Cindy hummed a tune and walked Ken over to a miniature church she had set up. "OK, now, church is over. Time to go."

I settled back and began reading *Interview with Merlin,* a Delores Macuccho book that I had wrapped up in a Tulsa Tomcats schoolbook cover. Delores's book was slightly smaller than the Eddings one, so it fit. Gray was right about her. She was one of the best writers I had ever read. In this book Merlin was combating a bastard brother who was half vampire and half elf. The brother was totally mesmerizing and Merlin almost succumbed; I could feel it happening. It was so convincing and scary, like a bad dream where every limb seems to weigh a ton.

I had been so absorbed in my reading that I hadn't been listening to the girls, but suddenly I caught a word or two and looked up. What had happened to Barbie?

"You are bad! Bad! Bad!" Cindy's thin face was twisted. "This is our club and—"

"What's the name of the club again?" Weesie asked.

"Mothers Against Satan."

"We can call ourselves M.A.S.," Weesie said.

Cindy looked perplexed. "Isn't that something to do with Catholics—mass?"

Weesie looked up at me. "Is that right, Harper? Is mass something for Catholics?"

"Yes," I said. "It's what they call their church services."

"Well, we don't want anything to do with Catholics," Cindy said in a low voice. "No, we hate, hate, hate Catholics." With each "hate" she slammed the snarly-haired Barbie down on the carpet. I just stared. This was scarier than anything I had ever read, including Delores Macuccho's *The Witch's Therapist, Vampire Fetus,* and *Interview with Merlin.*

"Why do you hate them?" I asked.

"We just do," Cindy said in a little-girl voice as she slipped the Barbie with the good hair out of the gold lamé evening gown and into an aerobic exercise leotard. "We hate them and Jews and niggers. And, let's see, who else?"

"But why?" I asked. There must have been

something in my voice, for Cindy stopped what she was doing and looked up at me.

"Are you a communist or something?"

I couldn't take another minute. I got up and walked back into the kitchen to see if Mom was ready to go.

16

SOMETHING
WEIRD—THAT'S ME

I didn't know what to do about Weesie and that disgusting little kid. It seems that when we came to Spoonwood we had all, except for Dad, found a friend for the first time in a long while. I found Gray, Weesie found Cindy, and Mom found Gina.

To me it was fairly obvious that I got the best deal with Gray. But Mom really did like Gina. Gina made life easy. Don't go to Clip 'N' Curl; go to The Haircut Place. Don't buy Softie frozen milkshakes; they go gummy in the freezer. Don't let Weesie play with G.I. Joe; it mixes up her femininity. Stick with Barbie. You shouldn't wear red lipstick; it's overpowering. Pink is your color.

Never wear navy, just on general principle. Gina had an opinion about everything and was ready to sling it at anybody who would listen. And Mom listened. What she didn't like hearing, she just didn't think about.

In the car it all just got to me and I couldn't stop myself. I really let Cindy have it.

"Mom, quit saying Cindy's just a kid. You should have heard the list of people she hates."

"You take life too seriously, Harper. It's all that reading you do."

That really made me steam. "It is not the reading, Mom. It's hearing little brats like Cindy say they hate Jews, Catholics, and black people. Except she actually said 'niggers.' I didn't read that, I heard it."

"Don't sass me." I knew exactly what was coming next: the two most hated words. There they were, right on schedule. "Young lady, you are the one full of hate. Listen to yourself talk. The Allmans have been wonderful to us."

"Yeah, I really like Cindy," Weesie piped up. Standard operating procedure. When one kid is getting grief from a parent the other one decides to be goody-two-shoes.

"Why? Why do you like her?" I turned around

and faced Weesie in the backseat. "She never lets you play with the good Barbie. She never shares. She bosses you around till kingdom come."

Mom swerved the car off onto the shoulder of the road and stopped. "I shall not have swearing in this car!" She was shaking her finger at me the way Dad had at Gammy long ago. It was very disturbing.

"But she does boss Weesie around all the time; Weesie never gets to make a decision."

"Weesie has a very nice playmate in Cindy. Weesie is just being nice. What do you call it? Accommodating."

"Weesie is being a patsy."

"I don't know what you mean by that, Harper, but being nice and accommodating is going to get you a lot further in life than being stubborn. Not everybody needs to be the boss."

I didn't have to hear the words anymore. I understood that it was easier to give up if push came to shove, if snarly-haired Barbie came to pretty-haired Barbie, if Clip 'N' Curl came to The Haircut Place. I had never thought of myself as being particularly stubborn before, but it was right then, pulled off the road, that I started to sense that I might be on a collision course with my own family. I thought back to the time in South Dakota. Maybe my mom saw back then this crash in our future, and that was why the sadness never left her eyes.

I decided not to say anything more about it. Mom clearly did not want to listen to me talk about the Allmans. School was starting the very next day. I wouldn't have to be around my family that much. One good thing was that the first time my mom ever met Gray, when he dropped by the Roadmaster one day, she did seem to like him. She thought he was very polite and was glad that he didn't dress punk or anything like that. And I thought he was OK with my dad. Gray asked a lot of good questions about the Roadmaster— miles per gallon of gas, stuff about the generator and BTUs. Dad and Mom seemed impressed. But I could never really be too sure of anything because from that day on, the day we picked up Weesie at Cindy's, it felt as though my own family had become a minefield.

When we got home Dad was there. "That fellow Gray called you. Is he a boyfriend or something?"

"What?" I gasped.

"I said, is he a boyfriend or something?"

I was tempted to say that Gray was "or something," but all I said was, "Look, Dad, he's just a friend."

"Well, I just think you're too young to be dating and wearing lipstick."

"I'm not wearing lipstick." I was totally confused. What was Dad seeing when he looked at me? I mean, I was standing there in a pair of cutoffs. I didn't even own a lipstick, or any makeup for that matter.

"I just want to know what you're doing over there."

It wasn't my imagination. He made it sound terrible, like there was something dark and hidden going on, which was ridiculous because Gray lived in a light, airy house filled with plants and sunlight and a gerbil that liked aerobics.

"Oh, Hank, don't get worked up," Mom said.

"I just want to know what's going on over there."

Should I tell my dad we sat in eighteen inches of water in Gray's swimming pool reading Delores Macuccho and eating Popsicles? Or that sometimes we watched his mom do aerobics, or we did games on his computer? Should I tell him that I cured Gerbil Jane?

"Well, we don't play Barbies," I said.

"Is she being fresh, Beth?" My dad swiveled around and looked at my mom.

"Harper, don't be fresh, honey."

"Mom . . . Mom," I sputtered. I couldn't believe she had said that. An hour ago I had watched Cindy and Weesie put words in their Barbies' mouths and move them around on the carpet. Now my dad had put words in my mom's mouth. "I'm not being fresh," I said.

"Well, just tell Dad what you do over there." An edge had crept into her voice.

"We talk, we hang out."

"Are his parents there when you are?" Dad asked.

"Sometimes."

"I thought his mother worked," Mom said.

"She does, but she gets off early because she starts early." They kept hammering away with the questions.

"She's an operator for the phone company?" my dad asked.

"No. She's a lineperson."

"You mean she climbs poles?" Dad asked.

"Yeah."

"Kind of weird."

That was all he said, but something crumpled in me at that moment. I knew that I could never again be really comfortable in my own family. I had become something weird. Someone who didn't wear lipstick but looked as if she did; who seemed fresh but was just confused, who sounded stubborn but was really scared to death.

"I have a stomachache." I really did, and that was all I could think to say.

I walked out of the Roadmaster. I wanted to use the pay phone at the Laundromat to talk to Gray in privacy. I had to see him.

"Please, please be home," I muttered as the phone rang.

"Hello there, folks! It's time for Headline Bingo. The publication we are featuring today is the *National Enquirer*. Here's how to play the game. From the words given in this message make up a sensational, sex-sational headline. First prize is a trip to Las Vegas. Second prize is a pool party at the Willettes' for pygmies—and that is your first word, folks, 'pygmies.' Now listen to the rest of the list—dictator, splits, hideaway, sexpot, heartless Mom, bimbo, Princess Di, blasts, escapes, lusts, explodes. Remember, folks, prepositions are free, don't forget the pygmies, and most important, political correctness gets you nowhere in this game."

"Shoot, Gray, I wish you were there. This is

not a pygmy. It's Harper, calling from a family of mental dwarfs—I am desperate. I am ready to explode, implode, split. My dad is a dictator. Good-bye." I hung up.

I found out later that Gray's mom had taken him shopping for clothes to wear on the first day of school. He looked totally cool. Doc Martens, black jeans, and another one of his astronomy T-shirts with a really neat silk screen of the Milky Way and the words, "Earth—we are inhabitants of a small planet on the edge of a minor galaxy."

The best thing of all was that Gray and I were in the same class. Gray said that Ms. DeSoto was the best of the three eighth-grade teachers. The thought of being able to be in the same classroom for one whole year with a good friend like Gray and a great teacher was pure bliss. I thought I could put up with just about anything my parents dealt out because all the rest would be OK.

And it was OK for a good long while. I stepped carefully through the minefield. I couldn't stand Gina Allman, but Gina and Cindy were easy to avoid. My parents were not paying much attention to the curriculum in my school or the books I was reading. For F.A.C.E., junior high was not where the main focus was. There was more attention given to Weesie's elementary school. They were still using a reading series there. Also, Cindy's parents were involved as part of their preparation to take the schoolbook protest movement on the road. But whatever was going on in the elementary school with Cindy's folks did not concern me, or so I thought until one day about two months after school had started.

Cindy was over at our place with Weesie. They had gone outside after playing office in Weesie's room. There were papers all over; as I was walking by, a paper on the floor caught my eye.

Dear JEWdy Blume,

17

TALES OF A THIRD-GRADE NOTHING

Dear JEWdy Blume,

We read your book *Starring Sally J. Freedman as Herself.* This is a bad book. First of all the whole Hitler thing is really stupid. There is no proof that these Jews really died over there during that war. It was all just made up by Jews to get sympathy. My parents know this for a fact. And you have no business talking about Jewish angels. There is no such thing. We thought you were smarter than that, JEWdy Blume.

Sincerely,
Cindy Allman
and Louisa Jessup

I felt my throat close up and a terrible feeling grow in the pit of my stomach. Gina had just driven up to get Cindy. I felt almost murderous when I looked out the window and saw Gina bending over and tousling Weesie's hair. It made my skin crawl. Mom and Dad weren't there, so Gina called inside to tell me she was taking Cindy. I could hardly stand to go to the door to say good-bye. As soon as they drove away, I called Weesie in.

"Weesie, what in the world is this?" I held out the paper.

"A letter to Judy Blume."

"Why are you spelling her name this way? This is so mean. Weesie, this letter is the worst thing I have ever seen."

"Don't get so upset."

"Don't get upset! Weesie, this is hateful, ugly."

"Well, Cindy's right. Judy Blume has no business writing about Christian things. She's a Jew."

"Weesie—that is the most un-Christian thing I have ever heard anybody say. I can't believe this. Don't you think for yourself at all anymore?"

"Of course I do."

"Well, think, think how much you loved all

those Judy Blume books. Think how you felt sorry for Peter when Fudgie walked off with his pet turtle; think about all those left-out feelings that Freddy felt in *The One in the Middle Is the Green Kangaroo*. And remember Andrew in *Freckle Juice* and how mean those kids were to Linda in *Blubber*? I remember you crying just last summer when I was reading *Blubber* to you. Weesie, what's become of you that you could write this awful letter to someone who's made you feel such real feelings, whose writing made you cry?"

One corner of Weesie's mouth tucked in as she swallowed and looked down at her feet. Her mouth moved around as if she were biting it from the inside.

"I'm . . . I'm sorry. . . ." she whispered. Then she flung her arms around my waist and sobbed. "She makes me be mean."

Everybody thinks it's the other guy who makes them be mean, but I wasn't going to lecture her now. I just said, "Well, don't let her. You're a neat person. You're smart and cute and nice, and you don't have a mean bone in your body."

"But she's my friend."

"That's not being a good friend, Weesie. If she's really your friend she wouldn't make you do stuff like this."

"What should I do?"

"Tear up the letter."

"But she has the good copy. She was going to send it."

"Well, tell her you don't want your name on it."

"How can I?"

"You can, and if you won't, I will."

Even if I called up and said Weesie's name should come off the letter, I just bet Cindy would never do it. So I decided that Weesie and I should walk over to Cindy's house, though it was a long walk, and Weesie would very politely demand that she be allowed to remove her name from the letter. And I would try to persuade Cindy not to send it at all.

So that is what we did. We removed Weesie's name. But Cindy, infinitely gracious child that she was, felt compelled to show us a table in her mom's sewing room where there was a whole stack of letters that her mom and dad had written to at least thirty authors and publishers.

"They all write dirty books," Cindy said smugly. "And if you don't want to be a part of God's work, Weesie, well, I guess that's your business. But I am not sure if I can still be your friend."

I felt Weesie reach for my hand. "Come on, Weesie, let's get out of here. You can find better friends."

I delivered Weesie back home and headed over to Gray's. I was going to help him make a cake for his mom's birthday. It was only three o'clock but the day had been too long.

18

A Solemn Twilight and a Starry Night

"I don't understand it. Those people are really weird," Gray said as we slipped the cake into the back of the pantry. We had cleaned up and hid the cake away in the nick of time, just before Colleen came into the kitchen.

"Who's really weird?" she asked.

Gray looked at me. He knew that I was sensitive about my family. My parents had seemed so stiff and awkward the few times they had come to pick me up at Gray's, especially if it had been after dark. Colleen and Al Willette were probably the most easygoing people that I had ever met, but I think my parents had reached a point where they were suspicious of anybody who was not a part of F.A.C.E, F.I.S.T., or our church. They were shocked when they found out that Gray's family didn't belong to a church at all.

"It's OK, you can tell her, Gray. I don't mind." I watched Colleen as Gray told the Judy Blume story. Her eyes widened a bit and I could see a flush creep up her neck. She turned to me.

"Oh, Harper, this must be very hard on you."

"Well, sort of. I just feel sorry for Weesie. I think I've got to help her find a new friend."

"Honey, that's really good of you, but you can't take on all the responsibility. You're a kid yourself and should enjoy that. Why don't you talk to your mother about it? Tell her your concerns."

"That's hard. Cindy's mom is my mom's best friend, and I don't think my mom would think that there's anything really bad about Cindy."

"But surely she'd be shocked by this letter."

I wasn't so sure. Out of the corner of my eye I saw Gray give his mother a quick, nervous glance. Stillness descended on the kitchen. I looked out the window. A solemn twilight had fallen over the paper-thin leaves of the live oak tree. There was nothing to say, and I had ruined Colleen's birthday party. I had brought gloom into this light, airy place. I threw down the sponge I'd been holding, burst into tears, and ran out of the house.

"Come back, Harper!" Colleen called after me.

"Harper! Harper!" Gray echoed.

But I was ashamed. I realized then that Colleen knew all about the Jessups. I wasn't fit company for the Willettes. I might bring the darkness and fears of my family into theirs—all that I had been hiding and avoiding and pretending didn't exist. It all did, and it clung to me like a bad smell.

I never would have guessed the speed of Colleen Willette. I should have known that after all those years of climbing telephone poles and doing aerobic workouts with Jane she was fit. I was a fast runner but Colleen was faster. She caught up and grabbed hold of me, almost tackled me.

"My family is so weird! They are just so weird. You'll never understand." I kept sobbing that.

And she kept saying, "I know, dear. I know." She didn't say, "No, they aren't," or "We all think our families are weird." She didn't tell me that things would get better. She just said the best thing she could have. "I know, Harper. And I know it's real hard for you. But please come back to the house. Something will be missing if you're not at my birthday party. Please."

So I went back. I knew that Gray had probably told his parents more about me and my family than I had thought, but it was OK, because they still seemed to like me. I didn't feel so ashamed.

After dinner Gray and I went outside. Gray had said there was supposed to be a good show tonight, meaning stars. Gray was really into astronomy, and I was getting interested because Delores Macuccho was an amateur astronomer. There was always a lot of star stuff in her books, which is probably why Gray got into it.

We flopped down on the grass the way we always did and looked straight up at the sky. This night was good. Orion was climbing up there, and Gray said that if the moon didn't rise too fast we might have a crack at seeing the Pleiades.

"OK," I said. "Tell me that stuff about the Pleiades because I'm right at that part in *The Warlock's Needle.*"

"Are you in part two yet? 'The Womb in the Sarcophagus'?"

"Just starting."

"OK—you're right. The Pleiades is coming up. But there's one thing you've got to know before you read this part or you won't get the full impact."

"Don't give away anything."

"I won't, but if you don't know this it really lessens the pleasure of the horror." I laughed. Sometimes Gray had the funniest way of putting things. "See," he continued, "I didn't know this when I first read the book, so I couldn't appreciate how brilliant Delores is."

"OK, so what is it that I have to know?"

"The word, sarcophagus—this will blow your mind. If you go back to the ancient Greek, the word means flesh-eating stone."

"You are kidding! That is so wild."

"But it makes sense, don't you see? A sarcophagus is a stone coffin—get it? Flesh-eating stone."

"That is so creepy."

"It gets creepier, believe me."

"What about the Pleiades thing?"

"OK, the chapter title has already mentioned 'womb'—so you get the idea that there is somehow going to be a womb involved with the sarcophagus."

"Oh, I get it. Gosh, it is sooo gross."

"Wait, it gets better."

"Don't give away the ending. The womb has to do with that creature-kid of the warlock—right? I mean, she is a 'she,' right, and not a 'he'?"

"Look, you're the one who keeps telling me not to give it away."

"OK, back to the Pleiades."

"Well, all you've got to know is that they were the seven daughters of the Greek god Atlas, and their names were Maia, Electra, Celaeno, Taygeta, Merope, Alcyone, and Sterope—and they were turned into stars. Also, there's this gaseous cloud around Orion called the nebula, and the Pleiades are considered young stars by astronomers; they're thought to have just recently left the nebula. You know, in the last few million years."

"And Delores knows all that?" I asked.

"Right," Gray said.

I lay back and looked at the sky, which was speckled with stars. I hoped that the seven sisters would show up. "Delores is so smart," I sighed.

"The lady is awesome. She knows everything—astronomy, numerology, Greek mythology, gynecology."

"What's gynecology?" I asked. It sounded familiar.

"Harper? Are you kidding me? You don't know what that is?"

"Like an obstetrician, right?"

"Yeah, sort of. You know, a doctor that specializes in women and all their sex organ stuff. Anyway, Delores knows about all those things *and* she is an expert cook. She's written books under another name on the history of cooking."

"She is cool. No doubt about it."

"I sort of wish she weren't married," Gray said. "Although I hear her husband is a really nice guy."

"Well, maybe she has a daughter and you could marry her," I offered.

"Nope, they never had children. It's kind of a tragedy—I read about it in *People* magazine. She's had lots of miscarriages."

"That's probably why she knows so much about gynecology."

"Yeah, probably."

"Maybe she'd like to adopt me," I said pitifully.

"Hey!" Gray rolled over and propped himself on his elbow. "Not a bad idea."

"Don't be ridiculous."

"Well, maybe we should just write her and ask."

"Don't you dare, Gray Willette—I don't want anybody knowing about my weird family."

I'd have to watch Gray. He had this do-gooder streak in him, and he might tell Delores about me anyway. "But I wouldn't mind just writing her," I said. "You know, for the heck of it, like you did. Maybe we could write her a joint letter and just ask a few questions."

"Yeah. I've been wondering if the warlock's creature-child might be the alter ego of the vampire's nanny in *Blood Dementia*."

"That's a good question—gosh, Gray. That is so subtle, I never thought about it."

We waited another fifteen minutes for the Pleiades, but they never appeared. So we went inside to write to Delores before my mom came to pick me up.

19

THE KING OF PERSIA AND ME

Life seemed to go along uneventfully for a while, which was the way I liked it. I did have to be careful, of course. The Allmans were still very much around. I wished they would get their book protest show on the road and get out of our lives. But Cindy did not abandon Weesie as a friend, despite the letter episode, and my mom and Gina were as thick as ever. I didn't see much of my dad; he commuted to an office in Rio Madre every day. It looked like the cable television thing was really going to go through. Dad was meeting with a group of people to develop programming as well as working on the administration of other F.A.C.E projects.

I was enjoying school. Ms. DeSoto was great. We got to do neat things in science—we built electrical circuits and made mini electromagnets. Even my folks were impressed when I repaired the broken Christmas tree lights. I built a new string out of some old ones and put them around the windows of the Roadmaster.

For Christmas Gray gave me a nifty astronomy T-shirt. There was a picture of the Pleiades still trailing dust from the Orion nebula on it; the contrails of the stars were pale blue and magenta on a black background. It was really stunning. Under the stars was a quote from Democritus Abdera—"I would rather understand one cause than be the king of Persia."

We'd had a cold spell, so I wasn't able to wear my shirt without a sweater over it for several weeks. When the weather finally turned warm one day, I left my sweater at home when I went to run an errand for Mom down at the 7-Eleven. When I came back, I noticed the Allmans' car and another car outside. I came in to find Gina, her husband, Ed, and Reverend Dan LePage sitting at the table with my parents; they had maps spread out and stacks of stickers and flyers around. I said hello, put the milk in the refrigerator, and tried to escape to my room to do my math problems. Reverend LePage stopped me.

"What's that on your shirt?" he asked.

"Oh . . . uh . . . it's just a constellation, a painting of it, actually."

"Come closer, dear." That soft voice.

"I'm, uh . . ."

"Harper!" my dad said. "When Reverend LePage asks something, we would appreciate it very much if you would do what he requests."

"I just want to see what it says on your shirt."

Oh, great, I thought. Just what I've always wanted—every one of these dodos staring at my chest.

"It says," I said in a clear voice, " 'I would rather understand one cause than be the king of Persia.' "

No one spoke. Reverend LePage looked down at the table, then jerked his head up quickly. Behind his aquamarine eyes there was the glint of a challenge. I felt something tighten in me. "Do you believe that, young lady?"

"Believe what?" I said slowly. Something was beginning to dawn in my brain. I used to think that he used the words "young lady" to whittle me down to size, but that wasn't all of it. Every single person in that Roadmaster was a "young lady," including my dad and Ed Allman. They were all whittled down to manageable size, spellbound by the reverend. A T-shirt like mine would not go over well with a power freak like Dan.

"The suggestion here," said Reverend LePage, "is that we cannot understand one single cause in the universe. But there is only one cause for everything, and we know what that is, don't we?"

"Yes," I whispered.

"The suggestion is that we are poor without knowledge, that knowledge will make us rich, as rich as the king of Persia." The voice grew softer. "But you are already rich as the king of Persia, aren't you, Harper? Because you have faith in God, you have accepted Jesus into your heart?" His voice was a velvet whisper. "You know that these are the words of a doubter on your shirt."

I wasn't going to be rude, but I'd be darned if I was going to be a young lady. "Well, I think he was a very ancient Greek guy who lived long before Christ—so maybe he didn't know."

"Where did you get that shirt, Harper?" my dad asked.

"From Gray, Dad. It was a Christmas present." He and my mom exchanged a long look. I knew right then that I had lost her. She had crossed over.

"Brothers and sisters," Reverend LePage was saying. "I think we should pray for a moment. Harper?" He held out his hand toward me. "Please join us."

What was I to do? In three seconds all of us young ladies were down on our knees praying with Reverend Dan.

"Heavenly Father, this is your friend, your servant, Dan."

Ding-a-ling. I could hear a telephone ringing in heaven. Hope he gets through on the private line.

"Hear now our humble voices as we come to you as a family in Christ. Dear Lord, we know that the blood that your son, Jesus, shed for us was not in vain and that the blindness and the stubbornness of youth, all youth as they . . ."

Reverend LePage droned on about Christ's blood and stubborn teenagers and sinners, about the bad influences of rock-and-roll and ancient Greeks. I started to play Would You Rather and decided that I would rather be called a sinner by Reverend Dan than a dork by Gray or anything bad by Colleen. The prayer went on for a good ten minutes. I would also have rather been in a witches' coven in a Delores Macuccho book than here in this Roadmaster.

I prayed, *Dear Lord, I know I can't ask Delores to adopt me, but more and more I can't help thinking about it. Is it possible, God, that I was born into the wrong family, or that maybe there was a hospital mix-up? But I guess that is impossible. Mom and Dad both say I look so much like Gammy—Gammy!"*

The Lord certainly does work in mysterious ways—I had never thought about Gammy adopting me. Maybe there was a glimmer of hope after all. It made a lot more sense than asking Delores. I was so caught up in thinking about it that I didn't notice that everyone had stopped praying. I was still down on my knees with my eyes clamped shut, looking like a truly repentant sinner, just the way they loved to see me. Gina took me by the elbow and helped me get up. She patted me on the shoulder and said, "You're going to make it, kiddo." This was supposed to be reassuring.

That night after everyone left, my dad called back to my room and asked me to come talk to him and Mom.

"We think, Harper, that this relationship with Gray is getting too serious."

"Daddy," I said, but I was looking at Mom out of the corner of my eye. "This isn't a relationship—you're making it into something it's not. We're not like girlfriend and boyfriend."

"I don't know that." He leaned forward. "I can't monitor you every second."

"You don't need to. We don't like each other in that way." I was dying to say that Gray's true love was Delores Macuccho, and I wished he would marry her so they could both adopt me—forgetting for a minute about Gammy. I was getting upset. "Mom, tell him that's not how it is with Gray and me. We're just buddies."

"Buddies can change," Mom said, and there was not even a flicker of understanding in her eyes. Her eyes, no longer sad hazel pools, were shallow, reflecting nothing, as though a curtain had dropped behind them.

"Gina told your mom about a seventh grader over in Stockton who got pregnant," Dad said.

"This is disgusting," I raged, and slammed out of the Roadmaster.

20

A STRANGER WITH A FAMILIAR FACE

There was nothing I wanted more than to talk to Gray. I had to warn him. How would I explain it, though? It was so embarrassing. What was I supposed to say? A seventh grader over in Stockton got pregnant and now my parents are worried about me. The whole thing was sickening. Gray and I were just friends and this idea of my folks' spoiled it all. I was so mad and so lonely. My mom, once upon a time, had said that she loved me more than any government ever could. I wasn't so sure anymore—because I don't think she knew what or who she was loving. At least that is what it felt like to me.

It was getting late, but I didn't want to go

back to the Roadmaster. I wasn't even sure I wanted to call Gray anymore because I honestly didn't know what I would say to him. I walked over to the Laundromat, got a Coke from the machine, and leafed through some of the magazines lying around. The light there is always so harsh and unwelcoming. *Don't stay,* it says. *Go home.* But there was nowhere for me to go. The more I thought about it, the more I felt like a freak. Honest to gosh, was there something really wrong with me?

I finally did go home. My parents, sitting at the table drinking coffee, looked up at me when I came in. There was no anger in their faces; there was no sadness. The look in their eyes said, "Who are you?" I was a stranger with a familiar face. I could tell they had given up on me, and I did not belong.

As I lay in bed that night, I thought about that alluring word. To belong did not mean ownership. You were not someone's property. The "be" syllable was about existence: "to be" yourself and "to be" in a special place that no one else could occupy within your family except you. The "long" part was about the heart, a place in the heart where a family met and lived together. They didn't just put up with each other. They longed for each another. To belong was not a state of mind but a state of heart.

In the middle of the night I woke up. I thought someone must be baking. I had smelled vanilla. But the Roadmaster was still. Everyone was asleep. There was no smell at all. Nothing.

The next morning I could hear Mom out in the kitchen. I had a feeling that I had dreamed a lot about her the previous night but I couldn't remember any of the dreams. I crawled out of bed and slipped quietly to the kitchen. I wanted to see her, to watch her without being seen. Had she really changed so much? Had I really changed so much that she could not understand one atom of me?

The phone was jammed between her ear and her shoulder as she stirred something on the stove. "Well, I don't know, Gina," she was saying. I suddenly remembered Gammy talking about how she was shrinking up in her old age. She had to use a stool to reach the top shelf in her cupboard now. Was it possible that a heart could shrink? I stared at my mom's narrow back. She swung around and gave me a surprised look, then flashed a smile, the distant kind of smile you give an acquaintance when you pass on the street.

I got dressed, ate a quick breakfast, and was just heading out the door when Mom got off the phone. "Where are you going?" she asked.

"Melanie's."

"Who's Melanie?"

"A girl in my class. We're doing a project together."

"Oh." I was already out the door.

"I just don't believe it! Your parents are getting weirder by the second. You know what this is going to do?"

"What?" I asked Gray.

"It's probably going to make you have premature sex or something with somebody. They'll drive you to it, and in a subconscious attempt to prove them right, a very inside-out way of getting back at them, you will do it."

"Oh, Gray, don't be ridiculous!" It was strange; I can't even say the word "sex" around my mother, yet here Gray and I were talking about it. But sometimes Gray, with all his gab and charm, really did push things a bit far. I wasn't mad. I knew that sometimes he just talked to exercise his opinions, like running a horse. Had to keep those ideas trim and ready for the track. But this one was very off track.

"Don't be stupid," I said. "I've heard of peer pressure for having sex, but never parental pressure. No, the only thing they've driven me to do is lie—lie constantly. First it was just a cover-up for my taste in books, but now it's covering up my taste in friends."

"Well, it's sort of true. Melanie is coming over here to work on the bridge project," Gray said.

But we were definitely stretching it. And I really didn't want to explain to my parents about the Apocalypse Bridge Project. That was Gray's name for it. It was a good name for such a bridge. Mr. Dunlop, our math teacher, said that ours was the most daring combination of trusses and suspension theory he had ever seen in his thirteen years of teaching.

Every year Mr. Dunlop ran the contest. We worked in teams. The only materials we could use were toothpicks, glue, and string. Whichever bridge held the most weight won. Last year a team built a bridge that held 12.2 pounds; we were aiming for 12.5 pounds. First prize was a pizza. The contest was a big deal at school. There was a display in the auditorium. All the teams gave names to their bridges and wrote out placards explaining the structure. It all looked very professional. Right after lunch on the day of the contest, the weigh-in would begin. Mr. Dunlop had a special little bucket to suspend from each bridge and fill with weights.

Ours was a low-slung bridge with three tall towers. This morning we were planning to do the cross-bracing for two of the towers in order to express the compression load. I was learning a lot about bridge physics. We were really well organized. If an arrangement didn't work, before we dismantled it Gray took a picture with his Polaroid camera because the cross-bracing and the string work were so complicated we couldn't always remember what we had tried.

The next day, Sunday, we went to Melanie's to work, but I couldn't get there until after church. By the time I arrived, Gray and Melanie had already gotten our bridge to support 11.6 pounds.

"But we've run out of weights," Melanie said as I walked in.

"Not to mention that our bucket isn't big enough to add any more, and if we break this bridge now we'll never get it rebuilt in time for the contest tomorrow," Gray said.

I looked at the bridge closely.

"See, she's pretty steady," Gray said as he added the last weight. "I think we can get at least twelve point four." It was pretty much an un-testable question, but I really wanted to figure out how we could win this contest. I crouched down and looked underneath the bridge. "You know, if we did two simple trusses under here and cross-braced the lower part of the end pilings, I think it would doubly express the load away from the middle."

"It would be some insurance," said Gray.

"It'll cost money," Melanie warned. "Our bridge is the only one except for Andrew's and Jody's that's coming in anywhere near close to the budget."

"If you doubled the string you could use half the toothpicks," I said.

"That's an idea." Melanie nodded. She was the treasurer of the project. Every toothpick represented $10,000, and the string was $1,500 an inch. So far our bridge had cost $40 million.

"Let's go for it—even if we don't double the string," Gray said. Melanie and I looked at each other. "Hey, listen," Gray said. "It's a make-or-break contest. You win for building the strongest bridge, not the cheapest." He was right. So we went for it.

21

APOCALYPSE APOPLEXY

And we won! At 12.7 pounds the bridge came crashing down. Mrs. Cranston, the school principal, captured it on video and played it back in beautiful slow motion. So did KVRT, our local television news.

"Well," Melanie told the reporter, "We were aiming for twelve point five. I think we would have made that, but if it hadn't had been for Harper's idea to cross-brace the underneath part and add those trusses I don't think we would have had a prayer for reaching twelve point seven."

"Interesting that you should use the word prayer in light of the project name—Apocalypse Bridge," Marilyn Bennet, the television reporter, was saying. "Can you tell us a little about this name?" She turned right to me. I froze.

"Well, it was Gray's idea. So maybe he should tell you."

Then Gray started talking about how this bridge was so daring it would be either the end of the line or a revelation of something totally new—"a make-or-break bridge, in terms of its construction—you know, revelatory, kind of prophetic."

The bridge wasn't the very end of the line for me—it was the beginning of the end. You could say the bridge was revelatory in more ways than one.

I had taken our laundry over to the Laundromat that evening. When I got back, my dad was on the phone.

"If you will just let me finish, Mrs. Willette."

I stopped in the doorway and didn't even set down the laundry basket.

"I am just saying that although we know you would not intentionally try to subvert our daughter's faith, this is not helpful. So after careful consideration, we must insist that Harper not visit with Gray outside of school or go to your house. Good-bye."

"What?" I screamed and dropped the laundry basket. Mom came into the room.

"We saw you on television, Harper." Her face was flushed.

"So?"

"So? So, she says!" Mom tossed her chin toward the ceiling and spoke into the air. "Harper, everybody has been calling us up."

"About what?"

"About your participation in this blasphemous project."

"Mom, it was a bridge-building contest. It was toothpicks and string and glue."

"Harper!" Her voice snapped in the close space. "You blasphemed the Bible. You showed a complete lack of respect for the book of Revelation."

"I didn't even think up the name of the bridge, Mom."

"It doesn't matter. You are not to associate with that boy anymore."

This time I wasn't going to back off. "Are you doing this because you care about me or you care about your precious cable station? Who called? Who saw me in that news report?"

"Reverend Dan LePage, for one, and the secretary of F.I.S.T," Mom replied. "How do you think this looks for our family?"

"I don't believe this!"

"You don't believe what?" my dad asked evenly.

"You're trying to control my whole life. Most parents would be happy to have their kid hang out with kids like Gray or Melanie. They're the smartest kids in the whole class. They're nice. Everything."

"They share none of our values. I've just talked to Gray's mother. It's clear that she is very different from us."

"So is ninety-nine percent of the world. You cannot be going around arranging my friendships."

"You belong to us, Harper," my mom said in a low voice. I looked at her hard, searching her face, her eyes. This was not the mother who had said she would love me better than any government ever could. She had no hope for me. She didn't know me. But she and Dad did, they thought, possess me.

"I am not your property."

My parents did not say a word, but the meaning of their silence was perfectly clear.

A few days later I came home from school to find my mother sitting at the table with Ms. Forbes, Weesie's third-grade teacher, and another lady. I could hear Ms. Forbes talking in a quavering voice, so I stopped short of the front door and pretended to fix something on the awning of the Roadmaster.

"This is really a shock to us," Ms. Forbes was saying. "We didn't really expect that you knew anything about this and certainly had not anticipated this response to, to"—she began to stutter—"this, this terrible note."

Oh, no, I thought. Had Weesie and that vile little Cindy written another one of their poisonous letters to an author?

Ms. Forbes continued. "I am really not understanding this as freedom of religion. This letter is clearly threatening."

Just then Weesie came from the direction of the swings. I grabbed her and hauled her behind the Roadmaster. "Why is Ms. Forbes here?"

"Ms. Forbes is here?" Weesie asked. A worried look crinkled her brow.

"She certainly is, and she's pretty upset about some note."

"Uh-oh. The Jesus Club," Weesie said.

"The Jesus Club? What in the heck is that?"

"It's a club that Cindy and I started. We got this whole neat packet of stuff: pins, stickers, membership cards. Cindy's mom got them from Reverend Dan, I think."

"Will you show them to me?"

"Sure."

We came in the back entrance to the Roadmaster, and Weesie spread the stuff out on her bed. There were membership cards—pink for girls, blue for boys. There were application forms and cards with Bible verses on them.

"See, these cards with the verses are like baseball cards. You can trade them and everything," Weesie said.

None of it looked too harmful, but I could see how the teachers might not want the kids passing all this out in school. I had a feeling there was more to it, though. "How come you're in trouble? Ms. Forbes mentioned some kind of note."

"That's because of Cassie Wilkins. She wasn't

going to join. She said that her mom said she already belonged to a church. We really wanted her to join because if we sign up ten new members we get prizes."

"So she should sign up just so you and Cindy could get your prizes? I don't blame her for not wanting to."

"No, that's not all. I mean—she'll go to hell and burn."

"Weesie! She belongs to a church already."

"It doesn't matter. She should belong to the Jesus Club."

"Since when have you and Cindy become recruiters? Is that what you said in the note that Ms. Forbes is talking about?"

Weesie nodded slowly. "We wrote it, but for a good reason." Her eyes widened. "We told poor Cassie we didn't want her to burn in hell."

I dug the heel of my palm into my forehead. The picture was becoming all too clear. I could still hear the women talking in the kitchen. The other teacher said, "Cassie Wilkins came in from recess crying that day."

"Well, I certainly don't want Weesie scaring anybody. It was just an innocent little club they started, but maybe it got a little out of hand," Mom said.

Ms. Forbes spoke again. "We can't allow clubs other than those organized by the school to hold meetings or distribute materials on school premises, Mrs. Jessup."

"But isn't this interfering with Cindy's and Weesie's religious freedom?"

"They do not need a club to practice religious freedom, Mrs. Jessup. And we certainly cannot have children threatening other children."

On and on they talked. They had hoped, Ms. Forbes said, to avoid going to the principal or the Parent–Teacher Organization. That was why they had come directly to the two mothers involved.

Two mothers was right. I smelled Gina Allman all over this. Worse than that, though, was the turn I sensed was being taken by Reverend LePage's entire organization. They had found available tools in a couple of nine-year-old children. It was one thing to take your child out of class and say that you did not want the child to participate in a reading group that used a book you didn't agree with. It was another thing to send a kid in with the Jesus kit and use the devil as a threat.

Weesie did not understand what was wrong.

She liked the pins. She liked the membership cards that she and Cindy could sign as co-vice presidents and hand out to each member. It was just like playing office. She liked trading the Bible verse cards and winning prizes if they enrolled ten new members. In a way I felt sorrier for Weesie than I ever had for myself. She was just too young to realize what was going on. Her mind was up for grabs. I hated this. Weesie was owned.

Before I knew it, the Jesus Club thing had escalated beyond all imaginable proportions. My parents and the Allmans were on television talking about religious freedom. Reporters were coming to the Roadmaster, and a fancy lawyer from San Francisco kept calling. I heard the words "test case" used more and more. A legal defense fund had even been started for Weesie and Cindy.

Colleen had said I couldn't always be looking out for my little sister. How could I help it? Yet I felt absolutely powerless, as if I were witnessing a living death. In many ways, my own life was made easier. The focus had definitely shifted away from me, my friends, and the Apocalypse Bridge project. Naturally, I had not stopped seeing Gray. Colleen told me I was always welcome in her house; she and Al had never told a person to leave their home and they weren't about to start now.

So I just went along in a kind of holding pattern. Maybe I thought I could go sneaking around forever. It was really easier for everyone, especially me, if I led this double life. I became good at it—not just the sneaking around, but the acting like a piece of prize property any owner would be proud of. I stopped wearing the star T-shirt Gray had given me. I started going to F.A.C.E. get-togethers. I even offered my services as a baby-sitter when they had evening meetings at the F.A.C.E. office; I ran a play group in another room.

I won't deny that I thought about leaving, nor did I ever once forget that I was in alien territory. I wasn't giving in; I just got more clever. I could smile and lie my way through anything. I thought if I could just hang on and not rock the boat for a while, then maybe, just maybe, I could get both Weesie and me out of the whole deal.

Maybe my going along had been the depression before a hurricane. Then something strange happened, and the boat began to rock. I wasn't doing the rocking, but could I hang on?

22

SCARLET RIBBONS

We were all at the F.A.C.E office in Rio Madre. I was baby-sitting downstairs. Some other kids were helping me, and Weesie and Cindy were helping out with the toddlers. An outside group was making a presentation upstairs, and it seemed to be going on forever. Finally the parents started to stream downstairs, all talking heatedly.

I saw Gina and Ed Allman go over to Cindy and Weesie. "How'd you girls like to really help some babies?" Ed was saying.

"Sure," the girls answered. "What do we get to do?"

"You're going to perform a rescue mission," Gina said.

"What kind of a rescue mission?" Cindy asked.

I couldn't imagine what they were talking about. Then Ed said it.

"Unborn babies."

"Unborn babies?" Weesie asked, perplexed.

"Yes, babies whose mothers want to kill them," Gina said firmly.

I could almost see the gears shifting in my mind. She's talking about abortion, I realized. I could not imagine, though, why she and Ed were talking to Cindy and Weesie about it. It seemed very scary. My mom came up and gave me a squeeze. "Honey," she said as she pinned a bright red ribbon onto my shirt.

"What's this?" I asked.

"It's for the Ribbon Rally."

"What?"

"Honey," she said again. "You're no longer just a migrant for God. You're on his rescue squad. We're all going to the anti-abortion rally in Sacramento. All of us—men, women, children, grandparents—all Christians are going to march for this. We are going to block those awful clinics where they do the operations."

I didn't know what to say. I looked around

the room at all the little kids and their parents pinning ribbons on them. These kids hardly knew where babies came from, and now they were being put in a march to save them.

I wandered upstairs in a daze. The Scarlet Ribbon people were still in the meeting room. There was a lot of literature scattered about on the tables. A plump woman, her hair pulled tight into a knot on top of her head, was talking to one of the F.A.C.E people, saying loudly, "We are calling this our Summer of Mercy. We'll kick it off in this area in Sacramento. We've got the Women's Health Care Services as our main target. Look, here's a picture of my oldest and some of my grandchildren lying down in front of the police vans last year in Albuquerque."

"Ooh, gross!" A girl about my age was leafing through a scrapbook on a table.

"Sweetheart." The lady with the topknot looked over at her. "Those pictures are a little strong, but that's what we're fighting. So you better get used to it."

I don't quite remember leaving the F.A.C.E office. Going home in the car was like a weird dream.

"So when's the parade?" Weesie asked, her voice full of excitement.

"Not for another week. And it's a march, dear, not a parade," Mom said.

"Do we get to miss school?"

"Yes, I think just a day, so we can get there early."

"Will their stomachs be sticking out?" Weesie asked.

"You mean the mothers?" my mom asked. I couldn't help but wonder whether this whole conversation was striking my mom as very odd.

"Yeah."

"Not really. Most mothers decide to do this early on in their pregnancy. . . . Oh, look at that, a new miniature golf course. Maybe we can go there sometime." It was pretty clear that my mom did not like some of these questions.

"I still don't quite get how the baby gets in there in the first place, and when they kill it how does it get out?"

"Oh, Weesie, you ask too many questions."

Then why are you taking her on this march? I wanted to scream. I hadn't said anything since we got in the car. Weesie kept gabbing about the big "parade" as if she were going to a circus. Every once in a while she would say something about murdered babies and then in the next breath would ask some very basic sex ed. question like, "Well, how do the women know they're really going to have a baby?"

My silence was noticeable. Maybe my parents were hoping I would say something to change the subject. Mom turned to me and said, "You're being awfully quiet, Harper. Something wrong?"

I shrugged. Everything was wrong, and I was totally confused. My parents had not said the first thing to Weesie, or even to me, about where babies came from. And now they were jumping into this? My mother could never even face talking to me about my period or anything, until I told her she had to, until it was practically dripping down my leg. Now here go the Jessups linking arms and marching down a street because some women got pregnant. I really didn't see how this was the business of a bunch of little kids, and I included myself as a little kid right along with Weesie. I didn't want to think about babies, sex, or any of it. I mean, the kids in my eighth-grade class still giggled when Ms. DeSoto would read a poem that had the word "breast" in it.

I couldn't figure out my own feelings. I had

heard enough about abortion to know I was against it. I couldn't imagine ever having one. I couldn't imagine ever having a baby, either, even though I love babies. But why did I have to march with my parents? Couldn't I have some time to decide for myself? Did I have to make a big pronouncement? Kids can't even vote, so why was I expected to march? It made no sense whatsoever.

The worst part of all, though, was my own sister, Weesie, the one I feared I would never truly know. Could I ever save Weesie? Outside the car window, the lights began to blur. Two slick lines ran down my cheeks. These tears wouldn't stop. I knew that. They would dry up, but they would not stop, not for a long time. Maybe never.

When we got back to the Roadmaster I went straight to bed. I had been a fool to think I could swing along for a while and just roll with the punches. I felt weak tonight, weak and punched out.

What would Gray say? I looked out the window and thought of all the nights we had lain out on his lawn and watched the stars in the immensity of the night. The sky was clear tonight. Out my small window I could see Orion's belt and even a little piece of the charioteer. Its brightest star, Capella, hung in the corner of my window.

I took comfort in the stars the way Huck Finn did on his trip down the mighty Mississippi. *Huckleberry Finn* was tucked in the Narnia cubby. That afternoon I had read the part where Huck talks about looking up at the stars when he and Jim, the runaway slave Huck is helping escape, are floating down the river on the raft. Huck says, "We had the sky up there, all speckled with stars, and we used to lay on our backs and look up at them and discuss about whether they was made or only just happened." It was very comforting that night to know that Gray and I and, long ago, Mr. Twain, had all looked up and seen the same sky and its beautiful mystery.

23

DELORES
WRITES BACK

"This is the last straw, Harper! This is child abuse!"

"But what am I supposed to do, Gray? I think I am against abortion—but do I have to go marching around like a robot? And poor Weesie."

"I feel just as sorry—no, I take that back—sorrier for you than I do for Weesie. She doesn't know what is happening—you do."

"That's the problem."

"You can't march. I think maybe you should go talk to the guidance counselor and have her talk to your parents."

"Forget that. They'll just say they can raise

their own kids. They don't need any public school interference."

"They can't raise their own kids, Harper, and the sooner you figure that out the better." Gray's mouth settled into a firm line.

I wondered whether Gray was playing Huck to my Jim. Was I like Jim? As if he had read my thoughts, Gray said, "You gotta get out. You gotta leave."

"I can't," I replied instinctively.

"What do you mean, you can't? You could go to your grandmother's."

"I don't know. I just can't." Something tightened in my throat. Suddenly I resented Gray and all his opinions and pronouncements. What did he know about all this? What did he know about just picking up and leaving? He had a perfect family. Easy for him to talk. But there had been a time when my mom and I . . . I didn't complete the thought.

"Look, I gotta go," I said.

"You're going to have to do something, Harper."

"I don't have to do anything if I don't want to."

"Sure." Gray paused and looked me in the eyes. "If you don't want to."

"I just don't want to," I told my parents.

"I don't understand," my mom said.

"It's hard to explain. I just . . . I just . . ." I struggled for words. "It's just so . . . so embarrassing."

"Embarrassing?" My mom looked confused.

"I told you, I can't explain it. I just don't want to do it." I wanted to say it was like forcing a baby to walk before it could crawl or something. Maybe its little bones weren't ready yet. But I didn't know how to say that so they'd understand. I dissolved into mumbling.

"Harper," Mom started again. "If you feel that abortion is wrong, then you should . . ."

My dad broke in. "It doesn't matter how she feels, Beth. We are going as a family to this march. There is no choice here. She belongs with us."

The words lingered like an echo within me. Maybe Dad was right. Maybe this was part of belonging. Not questioning, just accepting. I did, after all, agree with them about abortion. Maybe I was making too big a deal out of the march part.

"Look, look, just forget it. I'll go."

"Good," said my father.

"Good," echoed my mother.

I could never tell Gray. I would just have to avoid him for a while.

I might have been able to avoid him if it hadn't been for Delores Macuccho. She wrote back. And, of course, Gray couldn't wait to tell me. He had Melanie call me up. Melanie told me to meet Gray in the science fiction section at the library.

He was there already, beaming and waving a magenta envelope, when I arrived. I had managed to avoid him for a few days, but it really felt good to see him again. It felt so right to be standing there in the stacks with all those familiar call numbers.

"It's great!" Gray bubbled.

"Read it to me."

"Read it to you? It's to both of us. Don't you want to read it yourself?"

It just seemed easier to have Gray read it. I felt suddenly tired, so, so tired.

"No," I said. "You'll read it just right."

"What are you talking about? You had me

cracking up when you were reading that part in *Huck Finn* out loud." But he could see that I really wanted him to read it. So he began.

Dear Gray and Harper:

Thank you for your wonderful letter and those really intelligent questions. Most of the time people ask me questions like "How do you research your books?" or "What kind of word processor do you use?" Or they blather on and on about my skewed vision of the world and my delicate psychological state, and then say that they are just like me and feel a deep kinship between us. But nobody has ever asked me my feelings about the stars or ever realized that I am totally down on astrology and up on physics until you two came along.

To answer your first question: I have always felt that astrology cheapens the great mystery of the cosmos. It was as if the people down here on this amazingly insignificant planet in a lesser galaxy felt that all the movements in heaven were exclusively for their use, and because of that astrology functions like a self-help book. I absolutely detest self-help books. They are the last refuge of small minds, and it is my belief that most of the small minds are those of the authors who write them rather than the poor, desperate souls who read them.

I prefer books that answer no questions but raise millions; that do not simplify the laws of nature but deepen the mystery of the universe. Thus, you are so on target when you ask me about the significance of Goolog. A lot of people think it has something to do with Gulag, as in Gulag archipelago—the terrible communist prison that Solzhenitsyn wrote about. But it is nothing so awful at all. It is a marvelous splinter, a subparticle of time. It is a wordplay on the mathematical term for a hugely large number—a googol, which is what ten to the one hundredth power is called. For the Cosmos of Aran trilogy, I am actually thinking in terms of a googolplex, or ten followed by a googol of zeros. This is indeed the sliver of time in which the worlds of Goolog can exist. It is the sliver of time before time, before the event that began the formation of the universe, before the protons, the neutrons, the electrons of the atom began their cosmic dance of expansion. Can you imagine? Do you know what St. Augustine said when asked what God did before he created the universe? He said that time was a property of the universe that God created, and so time did not exist before the beginning of the universe. The Cosmos of Aran trilogy takes place between the borders of time and timelessness.

You asked what my husband does. Will it come as a surprise to you that Fred is a theoretical physicist? Basically, and it is a very basic thing to be into, gravity is his bag. He quantifies it. So people often say, "Opposites attract" when they talk about Fred and me. They wonder what our common ground is, because they don't understand the astronomy and physics in my books the way you kids do. But you must understand that both Fred and I are fascinated by the hidden parts of the universe and how those parts work, and, of course, how and why the universe began. And then I try to step into the narrative of those first slivers and ask not how, but *what if* there was another universe that danced on the pinhead of time?

Yes, I know that many of my books have been banned by fundamentalist groups. Of course it hurts when people say such awful things about you. They would probably be very upset to hear that I consider myself a Christian and I try to listen in my heart and to love. Yes, I do believe in God, and Jesus Christ, and that Christ rose on the third day—because, after all, God created the time that embraces our own human narrative.

I hope this letter makes sense to you both. I want it to because I am so honored by your questions. Perhaps someday we shall meet.

Most sincerely,
Delores Macuccho

"I'm in love, Harper," Gray said, clutching the letter to his chest.

"Oh, Gray. She is the neatest person. I mean, I'm not sure I understood it all but it was like she was right here talking to us. She was so sincere."

"Harper?"

"What?"

"Harper, maybe you should run away to Delores. I think she would understand your predicament."

It was now or never. I had to tell him.

"Gray, there is no predicament. I'm going on the march."

"You're what?"

"I'm going on the march."

"Why?" Gray looked dumbfounded.

"There literally is no choice. We live in a mobile home. My parents are driving the Roadmaster to Sacramento." It sounded kind of weak, but it was true that the whole family and the house we lived in were going to Sacramento. "I belong with them," I said quietly.

"You do?" Gray asked. I saw the doubt in his face, and I would be lying if I said it didn't disturb me.

Something blew inside. I'll never understand it, exactly, but all this anger welled up and I lashed out. "Who the heck do you think you are? You come from a perfect family. Your family lets you do anything. Your family's house doesn't roll. Everybody in your family respects each other. It's easy for you to go around being high-and-mighty about all this—you . . . you . . ." I sputtered. "You're just so damned smug—all of you. Delores, too. It makes me want to puke. Why don't you just go off and marry her?"

"What are you talking about?" Gray gasped.

But I didn't hang around. I ran down the stairs and out of the library. If the library door could slam, I would have slammed it hard. But the door just eased back with a swoosh and a sigh.

24

HER NAME IS JIM

I couldn't believe I had said all that to Gray. Just trashed him. We had reversed roles. I wasn't Jim anymore; I was Huck Finn at his worst. It was like the time Huck had ridiculed Jim, and Jim, who thought he had a true friend, had called Huck trash—"Trash," Jim had said, "is what people is dat puts dirt on de head of dey fren's en makes 'em ashamed." I had tried to make Gray ashamed of all the good things he had: of his family, of loving Delores, and of the high hopes he had for me.

Well, it was too late now. We were on Interstate 5 heading north to Sacramento. We were all wearing our ribbons, and I felt about as rotten as was humanly possible. I was the real trash. Huck and Jim were both poor and uneducated, but Huck hadn't become trash until he had played loose with a friendship. He had betrayed Jim's trust and denied him human decency. I looked around at my family as we barreled down that freeway. Mom and Dad had played loose with Weesie and me. We had become tools for them, but hadn't they become tools of F.A.C.E and F.I.S.T and the likes of Dan LePage? Were we all trash? Is that why we belonged together?

We drove into in an RV place that was near the march's starting point. From the moment we parked there, I had the strangest feeling. I had the sense that little pieces of the world were trying to get my attention. Everything took on a kind of surreal meaning. If I hadn't known better, I would have thought that I was caught in the midst of a Delores Macuccho novel.

The first thing I noticed as I helped Mom get dinner ready was that outside, directly across the highway, were two blinking ZZs. The rest of the neon letters for the pizza sign had gone out. But those ZZs blinked furiously at me, and I couldn't quite place where I had seen them before. It was like when you suddenly remember a fragment of a dream that you had maybe a week before. The whole feeling of the dream comes back, even if you can't recall the details. Those two ZZs kept haunting me all through dinner.

And as I watched them, something began to jump around ever so quietly in my chest. It seemed to be jumping in time with the blinking —but it wasn't my heart. It wasn't blood pumping. I could almost imagine a little person, deep down in my chest, or was it my brain, hopping around, beating its fists and stomping its feet.

I knew who it was. Her name was Jim. And she wanted her freedom.

25

OH, HUCKLEBERRY!

It's one thing to want freedom, and it's another to wrestle with the notion of trying to actually get it. I still felt as if I was doing something wrong to even want it.

Our whole family went to a march strategy meeting in the basement of a church that night. The meeting opened with a lot of hymn singing. Then a man got up with two other people, a woman and another man, to demonstrate how to resist the police without getting hurt. They showed different ways of lying down in front of the clinic entrance and how to go limp when the police came up to handcuff you. You could tell they had a lot of experience doing this. There were a few more speakers and then the Reverend Dan LePage got up to say a prayer.

"Heavenly Father." The soft voice slid through the close air of the room. "We are all sinners, but we come to you in your infinite wisdom and pray you give us the courage to stop these poor sinners who go tomorrow to the slaughterhouses of this city to offer up the innocents."

It was one of the most heavy-duty, gory prayers I had ever heard. There was blood all over it. I tried to pray for courage to get through this march, because the idea of it was getting harder with every passing second.

I remembered Huck and how he had been so confused about helping Jim get his freedom. He thought he was a really bad kid for helping poor old Jim, because in helping him he deprived Jim's owner, Miss Watson, of her rightful property, and back in the slave times black people were considered rightful property. So he prayed to the Lord to make him a better boy and to help him stop sinning. And finally he just gave up because the words wouldn't come. He said you can't pray a lie.

And I realized in that instant that I was praying a lie when I asked for strength to help me march. What I really needed to do was just plain run. I thought about Weesie, like a little unborn baby herself, never allowed to grow up and have her own mind. I thought about how I hadn't been able to decide on my own about this darned march. I thought about the slave in my chest, beating her fists. So I stopped praying my lies and thought of what Huck said when he decided not to turn Jim in—"All right, I'll go to hell." And like Huck, I never thought anymore about re-forming.

Weesie was nudging me with her elbow. "Lookee, lookee! Over there," she said, and pointed toward the end of the row behind us. I turned and looked and just about fainted dead away.

There sat Gray Willette, and he was wearing a scarlet ribbon on his shirt like all the rest of us. My true Huckleberry Finn had arrived.

The plan was simple, a lot simpler than one of those fancy jobs that the likes of Tom Sawyer would have fixed up. And Gray was so smooth. He comes right up after the meeting and gives a big, warm greeting to my mom and dad. They, of course, are nothing less than astonished when they see him standing there with his ribbon on. Gray says he's with a youth group from the Children's Christian Action Coalition—I swear he made that up on the spot—and that they are having a lemonade and donut party upstairs. Could I come? Naturally, my parents said yes.

I could hardly contain myself until we got out of the room. "You are too much, Gray Willette. Children's Christian Action Coalition!"

"Well, I was thinking of saying the Children's Crusade—I mean that would have been more accurate, but I thought it might be a giveaway."

"Oh, Gray . . ."

"Don't say you're sorry."

"Well, I am. But I'm not going to march. I decided. I've got to get out."

"Music to my ears." And with that he pulled out an envelope.

"What's that?"

"A bus ticket—cross-country. You can go as far as St. Louis on one bus. Then you can switch there for Georgia, for your grandmother's."

"Not Delores's?" I said, and laughed a little.

"No. We have to get a little realistic here. You love your grandmother. She loves you. And you did think once about Gammy adopting you, re-member. For all we know Delores might be a total idiot—just because she writes good books doesn't mean that she knows the first thing about kids."

I looked at Gray. After all those years of being in love with Delores, it must have been hard to admit that there was even the slimmest possibility that Delores could be a dud in any area.

Gray had taken the money for the ticket from his own savings account—a whole summer of mowing lawns. I swore I would pay him back. The bus left the next day right in the middle of the march. Gray had figured out everything. The route for the march went past the bus station. A block before we got there, I was supposed to tell my parents that I wanted to go back and walk with Gray's Children's Christian Action Coalition for a little while, and then we would cut in through the back entrance of the bus station. I would have fifteen minutes before the bus left. We had been planning to carry backpacks with snacks and sweaters, so I would carry in my pack everything I'd take to Georgia.

It was time for me to get back to my family. I wanted to kiss Gray. A funny kind of first kiss it was, too. Not the sort you imagine. I just grabbed him and hugged him hard, then kissed him on the cheek.

I didn't feel like trash anymore, and I suddenly felt a lot older, as though I had been in a time-lapse photography experiment. Although I knew that the changes were inside, I wondered whether something might show and betray me. Would I stick out? Sometimes in the middle of summer when we lived in the Midwest, right around the end of July when the trees were a deep inky green, I would spot one tree with one branch that had a blaze of orange leaves. An early autumn had come for that branch alone; the rest of the tree would be going along according to the actual season, still green, full of languor and summer slowness. I felt like the branch—out of season.

It began to rain on our way back to the Road-master after the meeting. By the time we got inside it was coming down in buckets. Thunder rumbled in the distance. Mom and Dad reviewed the passive resistance pointers with us and then said we should get to bed soon. Tomorrow was a big day. The march would go on rain or shine, but we should pack some rain gear in our back-packs.

So I began with the rain gear. It was hard to know what to take. My backpack wasn't exactly roomy. Mom had a bigger one. Cool as a cucumber, I asked, "Mom, can I use your backpack? I want to take an extra pair of shoes because if these get wet they aren't so comfortable."

"Sure, darling."

Should I have felt guilty? I had been lying about everything else for so long that the lies came really easy. In a way it was as if I had already left. As Mom, Dad, and Weesie went around doing the nighttime things one does before bed, I felt like I was watching actors on a stage. There was an indefinable space between us, as if we were on opposite sides of an immense canyon.

I concentrated on what I should pack. Not much. A couple of changes of underwear, toothbrush, hairbrush, jeans, my king of Persia star shirt. I would wear a sweatshirt. I got it all in and there was still room. I remembered the letter from Rosemary Nearing. It was in the Narnia cubby. I hadn't read it for years, but it was a reminder for me of that time long ago when I thought authors weren't real. I would take the letter and I would take one of the feathers Wingo had just molted. After I had read that first book about how birds and dinosaurs were kissing cousins, I read a few more and never looked at Wingo the same way again. Parakeets have a rather spectacular ancestry, as far as I can tell. Wingo's feather was a reminder of how exciting this place called Earth can be, even though it is a small planet in an insignificant galaxy.

I didn't take the few books I actually owned; I left them there under the floor in the secret Narnia cubby. I thought of them as seeds, ready to sprout in the darkness. But I knew they would not sprout unless Weesie discovered them. I prayed that she would. I left my books for Weesie, and I would dream of her finding them.

When I finally climbed into bed, a full storm was raging outside. The ZZs of the pizza sign blurred in my window like fingerpaints in the drenching rain. Thunder crashed, and soon the lightning started, sharp cracks that zigzagged out of the sky. Sometimes great flashes would peel back the night and lay bare the bones of heaven. It was so immense and so grand. And Dan LePage actually thought he had an exclusive pipeline to all this.

The thunder and lightning finally stopped. A steady rain kept coming down, drumming on the roof of the Roadmaster. At about two or three in the morning, for no apparent reason, I woke up. I hadn't been dreaming. I hadn't heard any noise. Everybody else was asleep, but I was wide awake. I got out of bed, went to the kitchen, and opened the cupboard to the left of the sink where Mom kept the baking stuff. I reached in and felt around in the dark. Flour, sifter, rolling pin, baking powder. There it was, the thin glass tube propped up inside the sifter. There were two vanilla bean strings in it. I took one out, put the glass tube back in the sifter, and carefully wrapped up the bean in some waxed paper and put it in a plastic bag.

I tucked the bean into my backpack, right next to Wingo's feather.

26

THE BOOKBAT
MEETS THE OLD
RABBIT

The rain has stopped. We're out of Kansas now. The wheatfields have given way to something green that sails past the bus window. I can't tell from here what it is. As I said, with every mile I get farther away from Gray and farther away from all the trouble.

It had all gone perfectly, just the way we had planned it. I told my parents I was going to walk with Gray for a few blocks and dropped back. I looked over just once at Weesie, who was carrying a sign that said, "Love babies, don't murder them." She gave me a cheery little wave and I waved back. It made my heart hurt to leave her there.

Four minutes later I was on the bus. Twelve minutes after that the bus was on the road. I was there with my backpack, two changes of underwear, my star T-shirt that said I would rather not be the king of Persia if it meant giving up questioning, Rosemary Nearing's letter, Wingo's feather, and a vanilla bean.

I always check out the newspapers in the bus stations along the way to see if there are any reports of my disappearance. So far there are none. We cross the Missouri state line at midnight and I switch buses at two in the morning. It'll be another ten hours or so to Georgia.

With the first streak of the new day we cross the Mississippi and I am filled with such joy as I see the mist hovering over the still waters. It's as if hundreds of years suddenly melt away and the borders between fiction and nonfiction dissolve into the muddy waters of the big, old river. Perhaps it's one of those googolplexes of time that Delores wrote about in her letter, where a whole universe happens between the margins of time and timelessness. I can imagine so clearly a raft with me and Gray and Huck and Mr. Twain—and Jim. I can taste the freedom.

In Atlanta I change buses again and take a

local up to Rome. Then I have about a ten-mile walk along the river.

It's a fine morning for walking. I go about five miles and take the turnoff down into Blue Hollow when I spot a rabbit sitting by the side of the road. Still as a statue it sits. I think for sure I'll scare it away. But it just looks at me, casual as anything, then shifts on its haunches, lifts a paw, and scratches its ear. I stop dead in my tracks and say, "You can't be . . . you're not!" And just then that little rabbit leaps up, spins 'round and with a lippity-clip and a blickety-blick takes off down the road. I chase along after him, laughing all the way to Gammy's.

I can see from the top of the drive a wisp of smoke curling up from the chimney. Gammy must be baking; it's a pretty warm day and she certainly doesn't need the heat from her wood-stove. And then I see Gammy sitting in her rocker on the porch with her specs on and her head bent. I get within twenty-five feet of her before she notices me. She stands up real slow, still holding her book, looking over her specs.

"Harper?" she says in disbelief.

"It's me." The words come out kind of strangled.

"Oh, Harper!" She comes bouncing down those steps as quick as old Brer Rabbit himself. She flings her scrawny arms around me and hugs me tighter than any 105-pound woman ever hugged anybody.

She holds on to my shoulders and pushes me back a bit to get a better look.

"Oh, Harper," she says in that soft way, like a gentle breeze pushing on leaves. "Harper, you gave me a start—and here I am reading a spy thriller I got from the bookmobile, and real life sneaks up on me."

"Well, I'm here, and I'm real, Gammy."

EPILOGUE

Dear Harper,

It's been over a month and I think that all the excitement has died down now that they know that you're not dead, kidnapped, or joined the communists, but at your grandma's to stay. My mom heard Gina Allman talking to the checkout girl at the Super Sandy the day after your grandma called to tell your parents where you were. She said that Mrs. Allman sounded almost disappointed that you had only gone to your grandmother's. She was hoping for something worse. And she was really ticked that even your grandma's minister had backed up your decision to stay there. Mom said she ranted and raved about how this just encouraged kids to undermine parents' authority and all that crap.

I think your parents are a little bit dense; they still don't think that I had anything to do with it. I just plain lied and said, "Nope, she never came back to march with me." Feigning ignorance was the only ticket here because they would have got hold of me and pressured me into saying something that would have tipped them off about the bus— better for them to think you were kidnapped for a few days.

OK, now for some big news. Hold on to your hat—for literally here I come! You won't believe it. But guess who's going to Space Camp in Huntsville, Alabama? Yours truly. It's a long story, but the short version is I started missing you terribly, and the more I missed you, the more I missed Delores, too. After all, I have no one to talk about her to or to read her books with anymore. So I was totally upset. I started getting pimples. My mom said it was because my hormones were kicking in. But I'm not one for ascribing matters of the heart entirely to hormones—you and Delores are matters of the heart. I missed you so much I broke out in zits. It's as simple as that.

Anyhow, I was looking at the map and I realized that Alabama is smack dab between Georgia and Mississippi. The solution seemed so logical—like how come I never thought of this before? If I was to apply to that space camp they run I could see you both. Not only did I get in, but I got a scholarship so my parents only have to pay for my transportation.

Now get this. I write Delores. I tell her how I'm coming to space camp and how you ran away to be with Gammy. (And I told her why. I hope you don't mind.) Then I go on to say how we'd both like to visit her. Well, guess what? She writes me back. Enclosed is the letter. We're invited to stay the weekend. Can you believe it? Mom is going to write your grandmother to work out the transportation details when it gets closer to the time. So see you soon, pal.

Love,
Gray

Dear Gray,

Your letter moved me tremendously. Harper's story is very touching. But what impresses me the most is the courage of you two. It would be an honor for Fred and me to welcome you to our home. We hope you will spend the weekend. We have a big old antebellum house on the Mississippi. It's kind of spooky. I think you'll love it. Many of the rooms are just like the ones I describe in *The Witch's Therapist*. There's a nice little cabin we renovated as a guest cottage right on the riverbank. You and Harper can stay there or up at the big house. I'll talk to your mother about transportation arrangements.

Looking forward to meeting you both.

Sincerely,
Delores

Gammy had brought Gray's envelope out to the garden where I was picking pole beans for her. I just stood there like a total idiot for several minutes after I read the letters. I couldn't believe it. Gray and me, reunited with Delores on the Mississippi, Mr. Twain's Mississippi.

I remembered a picture book from a long time

ago called *Mr. Gumpy's Outing*. Mr. Gumpy takes all these animals down a river for an afternoon ride, and they're all whinnying and oinking, bleating and quacking, making an incredible ruckus. That was just like what I was imagining, only it was Huck's raft. On it were Gray and me, Mr. Twain and Rosemary Nearing, Delores and Judy Blume, Mr. Steig and Gammy (since she looks like him), Mr. C. S. Lewis (the Narnia fellow) and the science writer who gave me the idea of Wingo being a dinosaur. The whole kit 'n' caboodle, all of us floating down the mighty Mississippi in the long evening shadows.

And as the sky darkens, a bat flies into the night, its shadow against the rising moon.